T0287584

Miss
Demeanor

Celia J.

Teen Girl Detective

Miss Demeanor

The Case of the Long Blonde Hair

Created by Ed N. White

Histria Kids

Las Vegas ◊ Oxford ◊ Palm Beach

Published in the United States of America by
Histria Books, a division of Histria LLC
7181 N. Hualapai Way, Ste. 130-86
Las Vegas, NV 89166 USA
HistriaBooks.com

Histria Kids is an imprint of Histria Books. Titles
published under the imprints of Histria Books are
distributed worldwide.

Library of Congress Control Number: 2021940258

ISBN 978-1-59211-106-0 (hardcover)

Contents

Editor's Note

This is a work of fiction. Characters, scenes, and locations may seem real, but they are not. Any resemblance to persons living or otherwise is purely coincidental.

Celia J. remains anonymous so that her work within the community to solve crimes and bring the wrong-doers to justice will not be impeded by notoriety.

Celia J. would love to make personal appearances for book signings or TV interviews, but that also is not possible. She has considered a website but is currently too active in weeding out crime and completing her summer reading list assignment from school.

Chapter One

How It Began

I can't tell you my real name. If I did, then I'd have to… well, let's just say, it wouldn't be pleasant for you. I'm a Private Investigator. I solve crimes in my local community, mostly because I'm not old enough to drive a car. Also, I don't charge a lot of money for my services because I'm not licensed. And I don't carry a gun. But, I'm smart and as tenacious as a Bulldog, and I can keep a secret.

Before I tell you about some of the cases I've solved, let me tell you how I became a detective.

My mother died two months before the end of the school year, which left my dad with crushing grief and a very sad thirteen-year-old daughter facing an uncertain summer. I felt that I needed to grow up fast and be there for my dad. He decided the best thing for me would be if I were kept out of harm's way. So, instead of hanging with my friends all day at the mall, he enrolled me in a series of day camps.

I resisted at first, but when I saw the list of offerings included Forensic I and Forensic II, I was all into that. Last Christmas, Mom gave me a copy of Laurie R. King's book *The Beekeeper's Apprentice* and I saw myself as another young Mary Russell working with Sherlock Holmes. I didn't have a Holmes, but I did have a vivid imagination and felt his spirit guiding me into a life of investigative prowess.

With school out for the summer, but the first camp not starting until the end of June, I had plenty of time to prepare. I binge-watched episodes of CSI and a few old black and white detective movies on TCM. I studied these for hours while sitting cross-legged on the couch, sometimes without even a juice box or an apple to sustain me, watching with rapt attention. I couldn't wait to examine my first dead body.

That wasn't going to happen, but what did was a call from my friend Roberta to tell me that someone had stolen her bike.

"I'm on the case," I said, then lowered my voice to sound more professional and told her I would meet at her house in twenty minutes.

She said, "Why?"

"To start my investigation, silly, don't you know anything?" I made a "tsk" after I said that for emphasis.

She responded with, "What are you talking about?" And added a "tsk" of her own.

"Never mind, just get ready to be interviewed, I'll be there in twenty minutes." I hung up before she could say anything more.

Now I need some investigative tools. For years my dad collected stamps. Somewhere in the house, there was a large magnifying glass. Using deductive reasoning, I found it in the desk drawer where he kept the stamp albums. Pleased with that discovery, I also took a black magic marker from his pen-filled alumni beer mug on the desk and a blank sheet of paper. I intend to fingerprint Roberta and any suspects I might discover.

I put these items into my backpack, along with a can of baby powder, a small paintbrush, to dust any suspected surfaces for prints, a trail mix bar, and a bottle of water. I slipped the straps over my shoulders, said goodbye to our cat, Mr. Whiskers, and told him I was heading to my first case.

On the way to Roberta's house, I rode my bike past the vacant school looking for suspicious kids. No one was there, but again using my deductive reasoning, I figured that was because of the school vacation, and they were hanging out at the mall. I'll go there after I interview the victim.

When I got to Roberta's house, she was sitting on the porch steps. To me, she had the appearance of someone who had just suffered a horrible crime, she wasn't laughing. I parked my bike on the sidewalk and approached her with what I considered proper demeanor for a hard-boiled P.I. I thought I should have a cigarette dangling from the corner of my mouth like in the old movies, but that's a disgusting habit and something I never would do.

I sat down beside her and rummaged through my backpack for my notebook and pen. "So, tell me who you might suspect of stealing your bike?"

She answered quickly, "My brother."

That surprised me, and I asked for more details. "Why do you say that?"

"Because he told me he was going to do it?"

"He told you he was planning to steal your bike?" I scowled as best I could and got right in her face. "Why would he do that?"

"Because I broke his kite."

I didn't mean to say, "Ah-ha!" It just slipped out. "So, he had a motive." I counted out one finger. "And he had means, he lives in the same house." I extended another finger. "And the opportunity, you were still in bed." I extended the third finger and then announced, "Case solved."

She looked at me and said, "What?"

I ignored that question and took out the paper and Magic Marker. Then I said, "Give me your hand."

She looked at the marker and paper and said, "What's that for?"

"I'm going to fingerprint you. You're the victim of a crime, and I want to rule out your prints from those of persons of interest." I learned that term from my CSI binge-watching.

She made a face and said, "What are you nuts? There was no crime, my brother took my bike. Here he comes now."

I looked in the direction she was pointing, and Emmett was turning the corner and riding toward the house, no hands, showing off. He skidded to a stop and said, "Hey, Celia," ignoring his sister, who put a middle finger up against her nose as a show of force.

"Hey Emmett, nice bike. Is it yours?"

"No, it's dummy's." He nodded toward his sister.

Emmett went into the house, letting the screen door slam. I felt confident that the case was closed, so I said to my client. "Let's go to the mall."

She agreed, and we headed south, riding our bikes on the sidewalk. I was satisfied with the conclusion of the case, and since Roberta was my best friend, I waived my fee.

***

Sunday night, before camp started the next day, I made mac and cheese for supper. It was my favorite at-home meal, and I think my dad likes it a lot. Tonight, he had that faraway look in his eyes. He had that a lot after Mom died. I know he's still grieving hard.

I don't think I've come into my full grief yet. I cried my eyes out for days after the funeral, every time another memory would come in view, but I think there's still more buried inside me. When I get up in the morning, she's not there, always cheerful even as her cancer spread, and there was no hope. We talked about a lot of things, and she always said, "Ceely, I know you'll do great things in your life, I can feel it." She'd hug me, and I could feel her thinning bones through her robe. Her last words to me in the hospital were said in a whisper, "Do great things."

That's what I will do. I'll be the world's greatest detective. I know it. I excused myself from the table and my father's stare and went to my room to cry.

Monday morning, I packed my bag with an apple, a trail mix bar, and added two bottles of water. The course brochure said we would be provided with lunch and a snack, but as a trained investigator, I wasn't taking any chances. The brochure also said we would be given a CSI tool kit, but I wanted to be prepared with my own stuff, just in case, so I added a notebook and the magnifying glass which Dad said I could have. He didn't ask why I wanted it, and I hadn't told him about my first case yet. He's been distracted all weekend. I don't know why, but I'll get to the bottom of that mystery soon enough. I was also excited by the fact that we would be given a camp tee-shirt, which I planned to wear immediately over the Ed Sheeran logo shirt I had on this morning.

Dad drove me to the community college where the camp was being held, and I saw the group of kids that were there for the course. Most of them were older than me, and one boy had to be at least seventeen because he drove there himself. My deductive powers were already kicking in.

I gave my dad a quick kiss on the cheek, jumped out of the car with my backpack, and turned around to wave goodbye, but he was already driving away.

All the kids were excited as we grouped in front of two tables to register and receive our course materials. I was in the A-M group, where there were three more of us than in the N-Z group. I looked at that as a good start. We were given a name tag in a plastic holder and a small duffle bag holding the other items. I slipped into the new camp shirt and pinned my name tag to it, wearing it proudly like a police shield. The registration lady said we would get our CSI tool kits this afternoon.

The girl in front of me said her name was Billie. She was three months older than me, and we shook hands with the feeling that this was what professionals did. She offered me a stick of Juicy Fruit, but I declined because I have a retainer to straighten out a crooked incisor and didn't want to have a sticky problem with that.

Our group leader was a man named Bob Marshall. He said he was a former city detective and retired on medical disability after being shot while chasing a robbery suspect. I pictured myself running down a dark alley, dodging a hail of bullets, to make an arrest when the gun misfired, and I disarmed the perp and slapped my cuffs on him. One of the kids asked Bob if we could see the bullet wound, and he said, "Maybe later." We followed Bob into a classroom and sat down.

Chapter Two

Crime Scene Detection

O ur first lesson was on Crime Scene Investigation. Detective Marshall showed a scene on the screen at the front of the room. A man was sprawled on the floor in a living room face down, obviously dead. Bob asked the class, "Who can give me a clue?"

My hand shot up like a rocket. He looked at his clipboard for a moment and said, "Yes, Celia, what's the first thing you noticed?"

"He's left-handed, Detective Marshall."

"Please, everyone, just call me Bob. Why do you say that, Celia?"

"Because his watch is on his right arm." I smiled and settled back in my seat.

"That's an excellent clue, and based on my experience, that's probably true. What other clues can be seen?"

He was addressing the group, but my rocket hand went up first. "Bob, I think he was probably poisoned."

"Okay, Celia, what leads you to that statement?" Bob smiled back.

"Because, there is no evident blood to indicate that he was killed by trauma, not shot or hit over the head or something like that. Also, there's no apparent bruising or twisted position of the neck, so I don't think he was strangled." I hesitated a moment to add suspense to my voice. "If you notice, there is a coffee cup on the table next to the chair where he probably was sitting." I had more to say, but Bob interrupted me and asked, "Is it possible that it was only coffee?"

"Possibly, but not likely." I hesitated again for emphasis, then said, "Notice the contorted fingers and the arched back, the obvious signs of Strychnine poisoning." I sat back with a Cheshire Cat grin on my face.

Bob shook his head, smiled, and said, "I applaud your diagnosis, perfect, Celia." He extended his hands in my direction and began clapping, some other kids joined him. I tried not to show that I was busting.

At 10 a.m., the class was halted, and we went into the cafeteria for a break. The school had a variety of snacks and juice boxes. Billie and I took our snacks outside to sit at a picnic table on the patio.

"Whatcha think," She asked.

My head was swirling with all the information we received this morning, and my mouth was full of an apple fritter, so I just nodded and mumbled, "Uh-huh," until I could speak. Then I said, "I am so excited by this, I mean freaky excited. Totally freaky excited. I'm busting."

Billie said, "Yeah, it was pretty good." She was on her feet dancing some hip-hop steps.

"Pretty good, that's all you can say?" I was surprised at her lack of enthusiasm, then I went on to tell her about my first case, which I solved the other day. "Yeah, after dusting the area for prints and checking witness statements, it was obvious who the bike stealer was. I tracked him down, interrogated him, and forced a confession. The only thing I forgot was to read him his Miranda rights, but I'm new at this, I won't make that mistake again." Billie stopped dancing and stood there with her mouth open.

After the break, Bob lectured us on the chain of custody following evidence collection. I made notes in the Selena Gomez notebook I brought, chewing on the end of my pen between entries. Bob told us about the importance of this chain because any break in procedure could affect a trial, and a mass murderer could walk. That thought sent chills up my spine.

He put on a pair of purple nitrile gloves, then picked up a folded pocketknife from the table, placed it in the bag, sealed it, and stapled a tag with his name, date, and time onto the bag. He handed it to a kid in the first row and asked him to examine it, then take it to the girl at the end of the row and give it to her. The boy turned the bag over a couple of times then wrote his name on the tag, and I guess the date and time. He got up and brought it to the girl. She looked at it, and Bob told her to hand it to the kid behind her. She turned around and passed it back with a smile. I knew what was coming.

Bob slapped the desktop and said, "That knife was used to kill three people, and we just lost the case in court because the chain of custody was broken. The girl turned bright red and covered her face with her hands. I felt sorry for her, I know she won't make that mistake again. I was serious about my work and had no tolerance for my own mistakes. I hope I don't make any.

Bob talked more about the chain of custody, showed us a completed card on the screen, and said we would get an actual card in our kits. I couldn't wait to get home and make copies so I would have them available for my next case. He then talked about evidence collection and showed us a video of two suited-up CSI techs combing an actual crime scene. I couldn't tell if they were men or women because they were dressed in the hooded white Tyvek coveralls, booties, dust masks, and, of course, the purple nitrile gloves. Using my deductive powers, I determined that the techie using the HEPA vacuum cleaner was a woman. She was smaller than the other person and was engaged in what people think is a traditional female role. A role I would gladly accept until I proved to myself that I could work a crime scene.

Bob talked about the processing of any of the evidence found through various lab procedures and showed us a gas spectrometer, used to analyze the atomic particles in a substance for comparative purposes. I underlined the word spectrometer in my head and intended to Google that tonight.

He ended the morning telling us that after lunch, we would receive our CSI tool kits and study crime scene reconstruction.

When we returned to class, Bob passed around a Tyvek coverall. It was crinkly and didn't weigh anything.

Then he explained the use of the tools in our kit. Small metal tweezers to pick up threads and stuff like that. Larger plastic tongs shaped like two spoons facing each other, like Mom had for taking eggs out of boiling water. Bob said these were used for picking up soft items, and I thought about body parts, like eyeballs. He showed us how to use the thin plastic baggies by turning them partly inside out to pick up evidence, but I already knew that because I sometimes walk Mrs. Tingley's dog, and that's how I pick up the poops.

We had swabs and plastic vials, Ziploc bags, little plastic triangle markers with numbers, a plastic tape measure, and a plastic ruler. There was a small container of cocoa powder to dust for prints on light surfaces, and we could use baby powder for dark surfaces. I was way ahead on that. The kit included a make-up brush for dusting, which would be much better than the small paintbrush I had at home. Mom had one of those, and I'll bet it's still in her bedroom.

Bob showed us how to use a numbered marker and place the ruler next to it, so we knew the size of the evidence when we snapped a pic. He said many detectives used their cell phones to take the pictures before the CSI teams get to the scene. I can do that. The magnifying glass was smaller than the one I brought from home, but it wouldn't hurt to have two.

For the rest of the afternoon, we studied Crime Scene Reconstruction. We watched several videos showing the animated 3-D reconstruction of actual crimes. Most of what we saw was pretty tame. I mean there were dead bodies here and there, but it was only animation, and there was no blood. Bob showed us the system that the city police used and was able to determine the trajectory of a fatal shot, where it struck the victim, and where it ended up after passing through the victim's body. That was cool, and it included an actual picture of a bullet wound taken at the hospital and shown on the animation as an inset. That was my first bullet wound experience, but I knew as I pursued my career, there would be many others.

Bob showed several more videos displaying different computer models from different companies, but they all did the same thing. They allowed the cops to reconstruct a scene and move the pieces and players to get to the bottom of the crime. He compared these computer programs to when he started with the police, and everything was done with a marker on a whiteboard, or sometimes on a table using small blocks of wood and plastic figures. He then asked for questions, and even I was silent. My hand went to my mouth to stifle a yawn as Bob looked expectantly at me, hoping I might have a question. It had been a long day, and all the kids were exhausted.

Finally, he thanked us all for our attention and said that tomorrow's class would be conducted by Detective Lieutenant Frankel from the city police, and the day's program would be about fingerprinting. That should be good because then I would be more able to collect evidence in my community.

We were dismissed at 3:45 p.m., and I went outside with Billie to look for my dad. I was busting to tell him all about my day. Dad was nowhere in sight. Most of the kids were gone when I remembered that my phone was off because of class, and when I turned it on, there were nine texts and two voicemails. I scrolled the messages, and there was nothing worth looking at. I checked the voicemail, and he had left me a message.

"Hey Ceely, I'm tied up in a meeting, and I've sent Joe Ritacco to pick you up. You remember him, he's my accountant. He was at the house last October. He'll be there, wait for him. I may be a little late tonight, so I gave Joe twenty dollars to give you if you want him to stop at Mickey D's on the way home to pick up something or maybe order a pizza. I'll see you later, I want to hear all about your day. See ya, Dad."

"Yeah, see ya," I said that softly, but it didn't matter. Most of the kids were gone. I sat on the stone steps and took out my apple. It tasted sour, but I ate it anyway. My big day and he couldn't be there to hear all about it. I felt sick inside.

Suddenly. Bob Marshall was standing there. "Are you alright, Celia?"

"Yeah, Bob, just waiting for my ride. I had a voicemail from my dad saying he sent someone to pick me up. He'll be here soon."

"Okay. You did a great job today in the class, good work." Bob turned and left.

I felt better now. I don't think he heard me say, "See ya."

Joe Ritacco was there minutes later, he tooted the horn and waved. I picked up my backpack and carried it by the straps. I didn't want to cover the name tag I was so proud of.

He asked me a few questions, which I answered, "Good." "Yup." "Good." I didn't want to tell Joe about my day, I wanted to tell my dad.

He dropped me at the house, I thanked him, and he waited until I was safely inside. I picked up the cat, and we went into the living room where I sat in my dad's recliner. I told Mr. Whiskers about my day. It wasn't the same as telling Dad, and I tried hard not to cry.

I know my dad has a hard time with his grief. I do too. But I need him. He's distracted, and I don't know why. Maybe there will be an answer when he comes home. I didn't bother with supper, I just made a PB & J sandwich. I was watching Wheel of Fortune when he came in. He seemed eager to hear about my day and came in and sat on the couch, facing me. I levered the recliner upright and started to tell him, then I noticed a lipstick smear on his collar and told him it was a long day, and I was tired and needed to go to bed.

"He said, okay, tell me tomorrow first thing. I want to hear all about it."

I said, "Sure, Dad." And headed to my room with Mr. Whiskers in my arms. I lay there for an hour thinking about the lipstick and how that might become my next case.

Chapter Three

The Long Blonde Hair

In the morning, I had gotten over my pout and was telling Dad all about the first day. We sat across from each other at the breakfast table as I spoke between mouthfuls of Rice Krispies. He was interested and asked several questions. When he was done, I asked a question of my own. "How was your meeting yesterday?"

He fumbled and said, "What? Yeah, it was good. A good meeting." Color rose on his neck.

After I put the dishes in the dishwasher, I called upstairs to him, "I'll be in the car, Dad." I heard a distant "Okay," and picked up my backpack and went out to the garage. I had to work fast, he'd be here in minutes. I found what I was looking for on the passenger headrest—a long blonde hair with a dark root. I opened my CSI kit, and using the tweezers lifted it off the surface and put it in a small plastic bag. I didn't have time to write out the evidence card, but I sealed the bag with a piece of Scotch tape. I noted the time, and when I make copies of the evidence card tonight, I'll enter that and staple the card to the bag.

I really wanted to dust the car for prints, but there was no time for that.

I tried to think of some more questions to ask him on the way to the school, but I didn't want him to know I was suspicious, so I kept my mouth shut.

Billie told me that two kids had been moved from the A-M group into the N-Z group to make them more equal, but we still had the advantage of one extra kid. Bob told us yesterday that on the last day, both groups would investigate identical crime scenes and see which group found the most clues. I couldn't wait for that.

Today, we had fingerprinting. I was surprised when Lieutenant Frankel came into the room. She was a tall, dark-haired woman dressed in a blue business suit instead of a uniform, and she looked a lot like my mother. Instantly, I found a new hero.

She sat against the front edge of the desk with her clipboard and said, "Hi, guys, I'm Detective Lieutenant Beth Frankel, but everyone, please just call me Beth. She had a beautiful smile. She read our names from the clipboard and asked us to raise our hands when our name was called. When mine was called, I nearly burst out of my chair.

She told us that besides leading the instruction for us today, she would supervise the crime scene competition on Friday. I was determined to show her that I was the best.

Before she started her lecture, she removed her suit coat, and I saw the gold detectives shield clipped to her belt. She began by giving us the history of fingerprinting, going back as far as ancient cultures who pressed their fingers in clay to show that they owned stuff, or whatever.

She talked about several different people in the nineteenth century, starting with a guy named Sir William Herschel in India who had people give their fingerprints when signing papers for business. I took out my notebook, and she said, "I'll have print-outs available for all of you, so there's no need to take notes." I put the book in my backpack but kept the pen handy in case I needed to chew on it.

Beth ran through the history of fingerprinting systems developed in various parts of the world and talked about Sir Edward Henry, who was a Police Commissioner in London. In 1896, he set up a system that looked at all the parts of a fingerprint that made each one different. She said that the Henry Classification System was used throughout the world.

I was fascinated by everything she said and the way she said it. Everything was done with a smile, and I saw her as my mother. I saw myself as her when I grow up. I was perplexed. She told us that today, a system called AFIS held millions of prints taken around the world and could be accessed by any police department in minutes to compare with those prints they lifted at a crime scene.

She drew a ragged line on the whiteboard that looked like a saw blade. She pointed to the peaks and said they were called ridges. The valleys were called furrows. Then she drew a bunch of squiggly lines in a circle and said those were known as the whorls and loops. These are what make everyone's prints different from anyone else. I looked at my fingertips. She said that after lunch, we would pair-up and take each other's prints using the old ink pad method. She said most police departments today use a touchpad and computer to take the prints.

She turned to the whiteboard and wrote Patent, Plastic, Latent using red, blue, and green markers. Patent prints are the easiest to find. You can see them because someone had blood, or grease, or something on their hands when they touched something. The Plastic prints were easy, too, because they made an impression like if someone picked up a bar of soap. Latent prints aren't easy to find, and that's when you need to use a powder brushed onto the surface to show them. My head was spinning with all this information, and when she talked about various fuming methods, I had to ask her to repeat some of what she said.

She smiled when she looked at me and said, "Thank you, Celia, let me go over this again."

I wasn't the only one who was confused by all this data. Billie turned to me and mouthed, "Thanks."

We broke for lunch and went out to the patio with our box lunches. I said to Billie, "Wow, what a lot of stuff to learn about fingerprints, who knew?"

She tried to speak through a mouthful of sandwich, and it came out as, "Um, um." I took that as a yes. I almost told her about my new case, the one I called, The Long Blonde Hair, but decided it was too early to determine the crime. When I go home, I'll set up a computer file and give it number 002. My first case, The Stolen Bicycle, was already in my laptop under CRIMES SOLVED.

After lunch, we paired up and gathered around a long table at the front of the room. Because we had an odd number of kids in our group, Beth told Carl, the seventeen-year-old boy, that he would be her partner. I thought I would die.

At the table, we were each given a fingerprint card with little squares labeled for the proper fingers. Beth showed us how to roll the finger on the ink pad then roll it onto the card, being careful not to smudge. She had Handi Wipes for all of us to clean our fingers. She said to be careful doing the thumb because it is turned toward the fingers and was more difficult to get in position. After she did Carl's thumb and several fingers, she had him do the fingers on her right hand. When that was done, she asked if there were any questions. There were none, and we began to work with each other. Billie smudged my left-hand thumbprint. I made a face, and she said I had moved. I made another face. When she finished, I did all her right hand without a mistake and waited for Beth to inspect the cards.

She made several comments as she went around the table. When she got to Billie's card, which, of course, was done by me, she held it up for everyone to see it and said it was perfect. I tried not to appear smug.

The rest of the afternoon, Beth lectured us on lifting prints from different surfaces and talked about various chemical fuming techniques. One of which used superglue. I'm pretty sure my dad has some of that in the basement, and I can use my hairdryer to heat up the surface, all I need is a fluorescent dye and to get more information on Google before I try that. I might be able to get prints from his car if he sleeps late on Saturday. I was well on my way to becoming a private investigator.

At the end of the class, Beth told us that Bob would be with us tomorrow, and the topic would be Bloodstain Pattern Analysis, and something called Blood Presumptive Testing. Beth said the pattern analysis is something we know of as blood spatter. I was all in for that. She also said she wouldn't see us again until Friday when she would be the leader of our team in the crime scene competition with the N-Z kids. She said that we would elect a team captain Thursday afternoon, and I wanted that so bad, I could taste it.

Billie and I and another girl named Rebecca left the school together. Billie's mother was waiting at the curb, and Rebecca was getting a ride with some friend's parent. My dad was nowhere in sight.

I turned on my phone, and he had left a voice mail.

"Ceel, I'm running a bit late. Leaving the shop now, it's four-oh-five. I'll be there in fifteen minutes. I'm on my way."

That was better than yesterday, but I was still disappointed. I know my dad is busy, he owns a small machine shop on Summer St., and he would often call my mom to tell her he would be late for dinner, but I've got so much to say to him. I sat on the stone step and stared at my phone.

I didn't hear Beth come up beside me. "Do you have someone to pick you up, Celia?"

I jumped at the sound of her voice then gave her my best smile. "My dad's coming any minute, maybe you can meet him."

"I'd love to, Celia, but I have a meeting with the chief, and he is not a happy camper when anyone shows up late. With the afternoon traffic, I think I've got a problem." She said that with a sparkling laugh that made me want to jump up and hug her.

I stood up and said, "Can't you use your siren?"

She laughed some more as she was walking away, saying, "No can do, it's against regulations."

Just then, my dad pulled up at the curb, he had the top down. I called after Beth, "That's my dad. That's his new car. His name is Daniel. People call him Dan." She turned and waved to my dad. It's a start.

I dropped my backpack behind the seat and clicked my seatbelt before I said anything. Then it all came tumbling out. "That's Beth. She's a detective. I think she looks like Mom. She's very nice. I don't think she's married."

Dad laughed and pulled away from the curb, made a U-turn, and headed into the city. He said, "It's Wednesday night, how 'bout we eat out tonight."

I don't know what Wednesday had to do with it, but I was all in. "Can we go to Chili's?"

On the way, I tried to tell him about my day, also about Beth. It was hard to talk with the air rushing past us, so I said, "I'll tell you when we get there."

Chapter Four

"You'll like her"

Ten minutes later, Dad pulled into the Chili's parking lot, put the top up, and when we walked to the restaurant, put his arm around my shoulder and gave me a little hug. In the booth, I waited until the server took our order before I started speaking. I was surprised that my dad ordered a mixed drink. He usually had wine.

I explained all about fingerprinting, and he seemed to be interested and asked me a few questions about it. I showed him my fingers, which still had a little ink stain on them. I started to tell him about Beth, and the server arrived with the drinks.

I sucked up some Coke with the two straws and started to tell him some more when he stopped me. He said, "Ceely, I loved your mother very much, and, of course, I love you." He hesitated, and I held my breath. "I've met another woman, Ceely, and we're going to be dating. You'll like her…"

I know he was speaking to me, but I couldn't hear anything. It's like my world was muted with a TV remote. I stood up, a little dizzy, and said I had to go to the

bathroom. The tears started before I got there. I stayed in
there for a few minutes, leaning against the sink,
wondering if I'd get sick. "You'll like her," kept echoing
through my head.

No, I won't! I'll find out all about her. I'll investigate
her because I know she's not right for you. She's not
Mom. I washed my face and went back to the table. Dad
said, "Are you alright, your face is red?"

"I'm okay, I just started coughing, I'm okay now." The
server brought our food, and I picked at it. Dad didn't
notice. He ordered another drink and began talking about
the golf tournament that was showing on the wall-
mounted TV behind me.

I pretended to fall asleep on the way home, so I had an
excuse to go up to my room when we got there. I didn't
want to talk to him. I didn't want him to tell me anything
more about his new woman.

I had a dream last night. I went to the mall to buy a
pack of candy cigarettes so I could look like a hard-boiled
private eye. A woman was there who looked like my
mom. I ran after her. I called to her. The faster I ran, the
further away she seemed. Then she stopped and turned.
It was Beth. She opened her arms to me, and I ran to her.
She hugged me and began stroking my cheek. I woke to
Mr. Whiskers rubbing a curved paw against my cheek. I
was startled by the dream, wondering if it really meant

something for the future. Also, the thought that I would buy any kind of cigarettes made me want to throw up.

I checked the clock. It was only 6:12 a.m. I rolled on my back and cradled the cat to my chest, feeling his little heartbeat as he purred in my ear. I thought about getting up early and lifting prints from my dad's car, but I'll wait until Saturday when I have more time. Instead, I lay there trying to come up with a name for my detective agency and think of a strategy to find out more about The Long Blonde Hair case number 002.

I had no good ideas, my detection skills weren't awake yet. Instead, I went downstairs and made raisin toast, coffee for my dad, and chocolate milk for me. I put these on a tray and took them up to his room. I knew he was awake, I heard the shower running before I went downstairs. I knocked on the door with my foot. When he opened it, he was fully dressed, except for the tie around his neck, not yet tied.

"Ceely, what a surprise." He opened the door wide, and I put the tray on the table by the window. The one he and mom sat at on lazy Sunday mornings, still in their pajamas, to read the paper.

"I wanted to tell you more about my class yesterday, I was too tired last night." I fibbed. I wanted to get his reaction to Detective Lieutenant Beth Frankel.

"Of course, tell me all about it." We sat, and he picked up his cup but waited for me to begin talking before he put it to his lips, looking at me over the rim of the cup.

"Well, Beth, that's Detective Lieutenant Beth Frankel, but she told us all to call her Beth. She's very nice. She's pretty, I think she looks a lot like Mom." He put the cup down. I continued, "She explained the history of fingerprinting, which is really interesting and was done way back in ancient times for people to identify their stuff. Beth didn't wear a police uniform, she had a blue business suit, like the same color as the one you have. Oh, I forgot you saw her yesterday." I picked up my chocolate milk, and Dad picked up his toast and raised his eyebrows.

"Anyway," I continued, "We learned all about the different types of prints and how to "lift" them." I raised my hands to make air quotes. "Beth told us about one technique using super glue. You have some of that, don't you?"

"I believe it's in the cabinet over the workbench in the basement." He was squinting a little, now.

"I was thinking about getting prints off 'non-porous surfaces,' like in the car." I made air quotes again.

"No, try the refrigerator, and not with any super glue." He laughed when he said that, and I imagined he and Beth laughing together. Then he looked at his watch and said, "We need to get moving, you'll be late for class." He stood up. Interview number one complete. I could tell he was hiding something.

***

Bob started the class by telling us that Beth was impressed with the work we all did yesterday, but he was looking at me. Then, on the whiteboard, he wrote Presumptive Blood testing with a green marker and Bloodstain pattern analysis in red. He said, "When it comes to testing blood clues, it's first things first. Not all stains that look like blood are blood. Or, it may be animal blood." He held up a piece of cardboard with two stains, they both looked like blood to me.

"This stain," He pointed to the one on the left, "is ketchup that has been left out in the sun to dry. This one," He pointed to the one on the right, "is blood." They both were dark brownish-black. "Now, how can we tell the difference."

My rocket hand launched, "By presumptive testing."

"Thank you, Celia. We do that with the use of various chemicals." He put the cardboard down and put a swab into a small plastic vial of liquid. He swabbed the ketchup, then took another swab and did the blood. The difference was quickly apparent. Then Bob said, "Just to use a silly example, say someone has eaten a Big Mac and dropped ketchup on his shirt, then has a heart attack and dies. The ketchup dries, and the first team at the scene might consider it murder and search for a weapon. You can imagine how foolish they would look if they didn't do the testing. I know that's a silly example, but many strange things occur at crime scenes." He looked at us expecting questions, then asked, "Does anyone have a question?"

Of course, I did. "What chemicals are used, Bob?"

"I have a handout printed to give you after class, some of the names are long and difficult, so I won't bother with that right now, but you'll get the whole procedure in the handout."

I felt like maybe I shouldn't have asked that question.

Next, Bob went into the pattern analysis. "You probably know this term as "blood splatter." He made air quotes. "But it comes in many shapes and tells us many things." He put a transfer on the overhead projector, and we saw several examples on the blank part of the whiteboard. He continued talking. "Bloodstain pattern analysis can give us a lot of clues. Such as, where the assailant was, where the victim was, how close, how far. We can determine the "angle of impact" (air quotes), which can give us some idea of how tall the assailant might have been. Many, many things can be determined, but we need to be very careful with our analysis because

BPA, that's short for Blood Pattern Analysis, is not an exact science, and the courts are becoming more demanding about our submitted evidence. We need to get it right."

I pictured myself being called as an expert witness in a significant trial and providing the evidence that locked up the murderer for life. Then I came back to the moment and paid close attention to what else Bob had to say.

He turned to the whiteboard and wrote Passive, Transfer, Impact, then explained each. "Passive is something that has dropped or leaked in a place like blood drops on the floor, or a pool of blood around a body. I'll illustrate this with a gun crime." He put another transfer on the projector of a body and pool of blood taken at a crime scene. I was fascinated.

"Transfer is when blood on an object is then transferred to another object, like this footprint." He showed another picture with the projector of a bloody footprint on a carpet. This was not as gory as the first picture.

Bob coughed and then showed us a picture illustrating Impact and explained that there was a forward impact, which was a fine mist as a bullet entered a body and a heavier mist and some drops as it exited. I was glued to the screen, absorbing every bit of this.

Next, Bob showed a picture illustrating how strings could be strung from the drops to a 'point of convergence' (air quotes again). That would tell us where the shooter was in relation to the victim and even how tall the shooter might have been." He said that today, most department BPA was done with computer programs like HemoSpat. This was another thing I planned to Google at home tonight.

Bob continued for another half-hour showing us pictures with the overhead projector. Then he handed out the printouts and asked if there were any questions. Just like yesterday, we were all exhausted, and nobody raised their hand, not even me.

"Okay," Bob said, "Tomorrow, we'll review everything we've done so far this week. I have some exciting videos of actual crime scenes, and we'll vote for a captain to lead the group in the crime scene challenge on Friday. I wanted to jump up and shout, "Me, me, me." Instead, I said to Billie, "If you vote for me, I'll vote for you."

She turned to me and said, "Okay, but I think Carl will get it, he's the oldest." The air went out of me like a punctured balloon.

Today, my dad was waiting at the curb when we left the school, he had the top down. I looked around but didn't see Beth.

Chapter Five
The Competition

My dad had a new hat, it was one of those tweedy flat caps, and he looked like an English country squire. I made a mental note of that and felt there were other clues in his recent behavior that I've overlooked. I'll make a note of these things when we get home. I leaned closer to him to tell him about my day. He put the side windows up, and it was easier to talk. I told him about the blood stuff, and he seemed to be very interested. I told him about the voting tomorrow for team captain, and he said, "I think you'd make a great captain."

"I do too, but Carl is seventeen, he drives his own car, and I think a lot of the kids will vote for him," I said that reluctantly, but it's probably true.

Dad reached across and patted my shoulder. "Don't worry, Ceely, we know you'll do great things." I think when he said, 'we,' he was including Mom. I know he misses her, and he has a right to meet other women. It's just that it's hard for me to accept that right now, but I'll do what I can to make sure that whoever he finds will be like Mom. I don't know anything yet about the blonde, but I will.

While I made an omelet for supper and added cheese and veggies, Dad had another liquor drink. I think he's planning to tell me something.

We sat at the table, picking at our food. I was waiting for an announcement. He was building the courage to tell me. "Ceely, Karen is coming over for dinner Friday night." I knew it. "You'll like her." I've heard that before. "She's going to cook something special for us, she wants to get to know you. It should be fun."

Well, la de dah, didn't I know this was going to happen. "That's great, Dad, how's your omelet?"

"What? Oh, terrific, best omelet ever." He laughed when he said that as if that made everything better.

I told him I needed to prepare some stuff for class tomorrow and went upstairs after I cleared the table, instead of watching Wheel of Fortune with him. I don't think he noticed how upset I was. I took Mr. Whiskers with me and lay on my bed with him snuggled against me, softly stroking my arm with his curved paw. When we finish class this week, we have two weeks off before Forensic II starts and that will give me time to pursue an active investigation into this woman who I will meet on Friday night.

Mom's hobby was photography. She was good at it and taught me a lot. Her cameras are in the cabinet behind the desk in the den, and her darkroom is in the basement. I haven't been to either place since her death. When I start my surveillance of Karen, I'll have all the equipment I need to get photographic evidence of whatever I need to show my dad that this is not the right person for him. I'll see Beth again Friday in class, and maybe I can get her to meet Dad that afternoon.

Thursday morning, Bob passed out little slips of paper for our votes. I looked at Billie, she nodded, I nodded back. Bob collected the ballots and spread them out on the desk in piles. He said, "We have three worthy candidates, the third-highest vote-getter is Amanda." Bob pointed to the girl with red hair in the third row and began clapping, we all did.

"Next highest vote-getter is Celia." I knew in my heart that this would happen, so I was able to smile and wave as the group clapped for me.

"And the team captain is Carl." When the clapping started, Carl stood up and made an exaggerated bow. I looked at Billie and rolled my eyes. She made a face.

"Well, that's out of the way, now about today's lesson." Bob was in full teacher mode. "Today, we're dealing with DNA. I know you've all heard of it. Can anyone tell me what it is?"

Rocket hand launched, and Bob said, "Yes, Celia?"

"Basically, it's the stuff that makes us who we are." I was proud of my answer. Billie looked surprised.

"Good answer, Celia. Yes, it's basically a molecule composed of two chains of linear polymers and their nucleic acid bases that are, basically, the storage of our genetic information. I don't want to get too deep into the weeds, today's handout will have more information. Let me just say, DNA makes us who we are," Bob nodded toward me, "and everyone knows, we're different from each other."

He stopped for a minute to see if we got that, then said, "We use DNA to solve crimes in many ways. We can identify victims, and we can identify the perps with DNA testing. I think in the future, everyone will be tested at birth, and their DNA will be kept in a central file. It's a non-invasive test that can be done simply by swabbing the inside of the mouth. How many have heard of Ancestry DNA? You see it advertised all the time?" I turned around and saw that everyone had a hand up along with mine.

Bob looked pleased and said, "How many have actually used Ancestry or one of the other sources?" Two kids did. "Excellent. Those services give you some idea of your heritage, but in a criminal investigation, we use it to determine an individual who left a clue behind, a single hair or drop of blood, or…" Bob hesitated, I think he was going to say something about sexual assault but didn't. He finished his statement by saying, "Any substance that could come from our bodies." It was break time, and Bob looked relieved.

After the break, Bob showed us two videos on the two large TV screens at the front of the room. One of them showed the gel process where a DNA sample was placed in a plastic tray; an electrical current was passed through it, causing it to break into strands. The individual strands eventually are measured, and this is the genetic code that identifies each sample. It's like a bar code in the supermarket. The other video showed an actual crime scene and the techies collecting the evidence for DNA testing. These were interesting to me because I had a single blonde hair in a plastic bag, kept in my bedroom, and I'll get more samples of Karen Friday night.

It was cloudy when we finished the class, my dad had the top up, and it was easier to talk. I told him about everything we learned in class. He seemed interested. I told him that I was second in the voting for team captain, and he said, "Carl's, what did you say, seventeen? I guess that's to be expected, but you were second, and that's good. A lot of the kids must feel that you've got the "right stuff." he released the wheel to make air quotes with his fingers. Then he said, "Tell Karen about that, remember she's coming tomorrow night." I thought, yeah, like I'd forgotten. Then he said, "You'll like her," and I wanted to cover my ears.

Dad was in a happy mood and ordered Chinese to be delivered. My favorite is General Tso chicken, and that helped me cope with what was coming tomorrow night. Before I went to bed, I checked my long blonde hair evidence, and nothing had changed.

My dad was the first one downstairs in the morning. He was fully dressed, including a tie I had never seen before. Also, he smelled like some kind of spice had been sprayed all over him. My first thought was that he had an important business meeting today, but with deductive reasoning, I figured it was Karen.

When I was ten, my parents took me to Walt Disney World in Florida during school vacation, and we stayed at the Disney World Swan Resort, which was about a mile from the park. It was wonderful, and I remember my mom saying it cost hundreds of dollars each night. Then we would spend our days inside the park where I did everything. We ate in fancy restaurants, and Dad bought me all kinds of Disney stuff. When we were flying home, I asked my dad if we were rich. He laughed and said no, but we were 'comfortable.' I guess that meant he didn't have to worry about money as some of my friend's parents did. A month after my mom died, he bought the Mercedes convertible. He told me he just needed to, and

I think I understand. Is this why Karen is interested in him because she thinks he's rich?

In the morning, when we got to the school, I saw that Beth's car was in the parking lot, but Carl's red car was not. All the kids were excited about the competition and wondering where Carl was. I saw Beth talking to Bob Marshall further down the corridor. When she came into the room, she started by saying, "We have a little change, Carl is ill this morning and not able to come to the class." Then she looked at me and said, "Celia, as the second-place vote-getter, you'll be the team captain."

I wanted to jump up and yell, "Yes! Yes! Yes!" and pump the air with my fist, but I said, "Thank you, Beth, I'll do what I can. I hope Carl is feeling better soon." My mom would have been proud of my good manners.

Beth explained the rules of the competition. Each team would be taken to an identical classroom in the building with our CSI kits. Each room had identical clues placed in the same spot in both rooms. We would be given one hour to collect our evidence. Then we would return to our regular classrooms, and the team captain would write a report on what was found. The team that found the most clues would be the winner.

We all would get certificates of course completion, but the contest winners would also get a metal badge that said CSI Junior Tech. I wanted that badge so bad I could taste it.

When we went to the crime scene room, there was a lifelike dummy sprawled on the floor, and I nearly jumped out of my skin. I assigned four kids to look for fingerprints and told them to cover the whole room, starting with the doorknob. I had three kids scour the area for bloodstains and two to look for physical evidence like hair, or thread, or anything they could find. Billie and I would examine the body. I checked the time, 9:16. Go!

We stared at the "body" for a minute, and Billie asked, "Can we touch it?"

"I guess so."

She pushed it a little bit with her foot, and we could see there was a piece of plastic wrap underneath covering the floor tiles, and there was "blood" on that. I guessed it was stage blood because the school wouldn't put real blood there. I was pretty sure. 9:27

We decided to roll the body over, so we put on our purple gloves and turned it over to find a rubber knife underneath, the apparent murder weapon. Billie picked that up and bagged it. We didn't have evidence tags. I was about to stand up when I noticed a mark on the side of the neck that was almost hidden by the long hair. I pushed the hair aside, and there was a bullet hole. Wow! I looked at Billie, and her eyes were wide. "Let's look for a bullet casing," I said, and we began crawling around the floor. There it was, under a chair, nearly hidden by the chair leg. I bagged that and stood up. 9:32.

My fingerprint team split up, with two kids working the back of the room and the other two kids working along the windows. The prints they were looking for were simulated with small black sticky dots, and they covered them with Post-its when they found them.

The bloodstain kids had already found four places where blood drops were small red sticky dots, and Jimmy found a series of red Magic Marker dots running up the corner of the whiteboard.

My physical evidence team had found several threads, two long red hairs, probably from a stage wig, and a broken pencil. 10:04 a.m.

Beth opened the door and said, "Times up. Now you need to bring your evidence back to the classroom and write the report."

Chapter Six

The Winner

Beth gave me a police report form. The first thing we needed was the case name. Darlene suggested, The Classroom Caper, and we all agreed on that. Then we described the victim and gave him the name Charlie, age approximately 40 years old, Caucasian male. Height estimated at 6 feet, Billie and I did that with a tape measure, and I guessed his weight at 200 pounds because that's what my dad weighed. We described the color of his hair, but the eyes on the dummy were closed, and Billie and I didn't want to try opening them. We described his clothes and the tattoo seen on the back of his hand and noted that he had both stab wounds and a bullet hole.

We listed the suspect as "Unknown," but suggested it was someone who had both a gun and a knife.

We needed to summarize the case in 2-3 paragraphs of text, and everyone chipped in their ideas while I wrote them with my pen, wishing I had my laptop.

The form asked for any Testimonial Evidence, and I wrote, 'No known witnesses.'

Then I had to list the Physical Evidence, and my fingerprint team gave the location and number of prints found at each site. The bloodstain team noted the number of drops and the impact spray on the whiteboard. My physical evidence team found three threads, two long red hairs, a gum wrapper, and Billie and I had found the rubber knife and the empty shell casing. I think we all did an excellent job.

We put everything in a cardboard box and gave it to Beth, she would meet with Bob, who was supervising the other team and make their decision. While they did that, we had a pizza party in the cafeteria and were given ice cream squares after the meal. We were all excited to learn who would be the winner and couldn't wait for the announcement.

Bob Marshall blew a police whistle, and we jumped out of our skins. He laughed and said in a stage voice that got us laughing, "Ladies and gentlemen, lads and lassies, it gives us..." He waved a hand toward Beth, "great pleasure to announce the winner of the crime scene detection contest." He ruffled some papers in his hand. The winning team is... But, first, we pause for these announcements." He motioned to Beth.

"I just want to say what a pleasure it was working with all you guys. You all did a great job. There is a winner, but there are also no losers. I hope you all got a lot out of this course, and I look forward to meeting you again when we start Forensic II." She and Bob both started clapping. I was so excited.

Bob started ruffling the papers in his hand again, cleared his throat twice, studied the top page, put a hand to his chin, and started stroking that as if he had a decision to make. We figured he was playing with us and started booing,

Bob smiled, laughed, and said, "The winner, by only one clue, is… team Celia."

I leaped to my feet and started jumping up and down, our team all came together, and twelve excited kids began jumping up and down, screaming.

Finally, Bob blew his whistle and told us to line up and give the other team a high five. We slapped hands as we filed past them, and then Bob told us to line up at the front of the room. Beth presented the certificates to the other team and shook their hands, then she came to us with certificates and our gold-colored metal badges. She announced again that only one clue separated the two teams, and that was the impact "blood" spatter that Jimmy found on the corner of the whiteboard. We cheered for Jimmy.

Bob held up his hand and blew the whistle again. "As you know, Forensic II will start on the fifteenth, so you have two weeks off. Beth and I wish you a happy, safe vacation, and we look forward to seeing you all here again. Thank you for participating. Beth didn't say anything, she just smiled, and that was enough for me.

We all yelled, "Thank you, Bob and Beth," and clapped for them. We all hugged and said our "goodbyes" and "see ya's" to each other, and Billie and I walked out of the school together. She said she was going on a trip to New Mexico with her parents to visit her grandparents. I didn't tell her I would be involved in the investigation of Karen.

Dad was at the curb with the top down. He was wearing his sporty cap again, and I could see by the way his hair was trimmed along his neck that he had just had a haircut. He also smelled spicy. I guess he did that for Karen. I proudly showed him my CSI Junior Tech badge, which he studied carefully, turning it over several times in his hand. "That's wonderful, Ceely, wait until Karen sees this."

It seems like everything centers around Karen now. We'll see about that.

When we got home, the first thing I noticed was the cut flowers on the dining room table. When I went to the fridge for a water bottle, there was a bottle of champagne on the door shelf. Whoop de do, I rolled my eyes.

I took my certificate in the den and stuck it on the wall with tape among some of the framed photographs my mom had made. Dad said he would get my certificate framed, Monday.

I went upstairs and lay on my bed with the cat trying to figure a strategy for my Karen investigation. It was simple, I would bite my tongue and appear friendly and interested in her life. Mom always said, "You catch more flies with honey than you do with vinegar." This was one fly I would ensnare with my investigative skills. I planned to ask her simple questions, to avoid any suspicion and, of course, the glass she used at dinner would be kept aside when I cleared the table so I could dust it for prints. Once I had gathered the information about her, I would put her under surveillance and use one of my mom's cameras when needed to collect evidence.

With these happy thoughts in place, I put my earbuds in and listened to Selena Gomez.

"She's here, Ceel." My dad's call from downstairs broke into my daydream, like a splash of cold water. I went to the window and watched him greet her in the driveway. They hugged, but thank God, they didn't kiss. At least from what I could see.

I checked myself in the mirror as I left my room, my new gold badge was pinned proudly on my CSI camp tee shirt.

When I got downstairs, Dad introduced us. "Karen, this is my daughter, Celia, she's thirteen and just finished a week at a CSI camp." He looked very proud to say that.

Karen smiled at me, said that it was an incredible accomplishment, and extended her greeting hand.

I smiled back and said, "The pleasure is all mine." Something I heard on TV. We shook hands, and without really meaning to, I then scrubbed my hand on my jeans. They didn't seem to notice.

"Dan, will you help me get some things from the car." She smiled at my dad, showing a lot of very white teeth, but it was not a happy smile like Beth always had. It was more like part of her command.

Being friendly, I offered to help, but Karen said that was not necessary, and she led my dad outside like a puppy on a leash. She loaded him with two bags of groceries for tonight's "special" meal, then reached behind the seat to retrieve a small suitcase. "Oh my God, she's planning to stay over!" I had not anticipated that.

I got over that horrible thought because we had a lovely guest bedroom with its own bath and went back to friendly mode.

My mom always said there was some goodness in everyone, and I had to admit that Karen knew how to cook. I also assumed that Beth could, as well.

We ate in the dining room instead of the kitchen where Dad and I usually ate. Dad uncorked the champagne, and the stopper hit the ceiling as it exploded from the bottle. We all laughed at that, but Karen's laugh had a tinny, hollow sound to it, not like Beth.

I did admit that the meal was tasty and said, "That was the best Lasagna I've ever had." I didn't bother to cross my fingers under the table. It really didn't matter. After dinner, I cleared the table and stacked the dishwasher while Karen and my dad sat on the couch to watch TV. I think they were holding hands but I wasn't sure. I took the glass she had used up to my room. I'll fingerprint that tomorrow.

I made enough noise coming back downstairs to give them a warning and then went in and sat in the chair closest to Karen. "So, Karen, do you live in this neighborhood?" I also asked her where she worked, did she have any children, did she have a dog, and finally, "Have you been married before?"

That surprised her, and I don't think she was happy with that question. I could see that my dad wasn't. But this is part of an investigation, and I intend to get answers.

She responded coldly, "No, I have not."

One more thing I needed to know. "Where do you work?"

She handled this a little better. "I'm self-employed, Celia, I represent several companies."

"So, you're a salesperson?"

Karen answered that with her thin smile. "Manufacturer's Representative."

Interview over, I said goodnight to them and went upstairs to add comments to the case file then read from an Alan Bradley book about Flavia de Luce, the fictional eleven-year-old girl solving murder cases in England, before I went to sleep.

I was up early on Saturday morning. The house was quiet. I dressed and headed for the kitchen. Further down the hall, the guest bedroom door was open, and the bed had not been used. I looked out the window overlooking the driveway, and Karen's car was still here. I didn't like the image my deductive reasoning gave me.

Chapter Seven

The Mall, Karen, More Clues

I fed Mr. Whiskers, then myself. After an early bowl of Rice Krispies, I went back upstairs to work on Case 002. I dusted the glass and lifted several good prints of the Wicked Witch's fingers. I used the cocoa powder and saved the prints with wide Scotch tape. I put the tape on a clean sheet of copy paper, then scanned that into my computer file labeled, The Long Blonde Hair. I Googled the location of her office and general area of her home, although, I didn't have exact addresses, yet. I'll work on that when I see her today. I added that information into the file.

It was 8:15 a.m., and I hadn't heard a peep from either one of them. I briefly thought about surveilling them with a water glass held against the wall, but I wasn't ready to hear what I didn't want to happen. I called Roberta.

She was always up early, even on Saturday mornings, because they had an old dog that needed to go for a walk. When she answered, I could tell from the background noise that she was already outside walking down the sidewalk on Pembroke Street. "Hey, Robbie, wanna go to the mall today?

"You bet."

"I need to get a birthday card for my cousin in Ohio."

"Donnie?"

"It's Lonnie, she's fifteen."

"Okay, wanna ride there together?"

"Yup, I'll come over about ten-thirty."

"Okay."

"Ten-four."

"What?"

"That's what cops say."

She hung up, but I think I heard her say something like, "Sheesh!"

I toyed with the idea of making coffee, toasting bagels, and bringing that to their bedroom, but when I closed my eyes and projected that thought all the way upstairs, the image was more than I could bear. If they weren't awake before I left for the mall, I'd put a note on the kitchen table. My dad always wanted to know where I was going. He was careful not to helicopter me, and, after mom died, we had a long talk about responsibility, and he gave me some rules that I try to keep.

The air was warm, and there was no hint of rain, so I proudly wore my CSI camp tee shirt. I didn't pin on the badge, I thought that would be a little much until I completed Forensic II. Also, I still hadn't come up with a name for my detective agency, so I hadn't yet printed out my business cards. Besides the birthday card I had to buy, I planned to get some card stock at Staples. Last Thursday, I Googled how to make a business card, and got all the information I needed, I just have to decide on a cool name. In the meantime, I'll hope for more business by word of mouth. I'm sure Roberta is a satisfied client.

I put a snack and a bottle of water in my backpack, then decided to add my magnifying glass, just in case. I said goodbye to Mr. Whiskers, clicked on my helmet, and rode my new Trek bike that dad bought me when he bought his new car. Like his car, he was hoping to distract me from my grief. It didn't. Nothing will for a long time. That was one reason I decided to pursue my career as a private investigator, to lose myself in the pursuit of justice.

When I got to Roberta's house, she was sitting on the porch step, and her bike was parked in front. I was somewhat disappointed that there would be no investigation needed today. The traffic was heavy this morning, and we rode all the way to the mall on the sidewalk. We locked our bikes in the rack by the south entrance and went in to meet our friends who would gather in the food court on Saturdays. Maybe I can pick up some business here.

The kids all liked my shirt, and I spent half an hour explaining all about the course and told them about Beth. Jenny said that she wanted to join the FBI when she graduated from college and stole the spotlight for a while as she explained what she knew about that.

When she was done talking about herself, I said, "If any of you need the assistance of a private investigator, I'm available."

Mike asked me, "What for?"

I shrugged and said, "To investigate anything suspicious?"

"Like what?"

I rolled my eyes, "I solved a stolen bicycle case last week."

Roberta rolled her eyes.

Mike asked, "What about checking up on someone?"

I answered, "That's what I do best. I'm working on one of those cases right now."

"Who?"

"Mikey, don't be a jerk. I can't talk about ongoing investigations." I started to say more about that when

Marilyn arrived and showed off her new Nikes. I hadn't figured this age group could be so easily distracted.

Roberta and I bought a couple of Cokes and sat at a round table by the windows. She asked me about the new case I was working on. "Well, my dad has a new girlfriend, at least it seems that way. She came to the house and stayed over last night."

Her eyes widened, and she said, "Did they sleep in the same room?"

"'Fraid so."

"Wow!" She started slurping the bottom of the cup with her straw, then said, "What are you going to do about it?"

I answered, "Right now, I'm gathering evidence and information. I've already got her fingerprints on file, and I've collected a hair. She has brown roots. I interrogated her last night for more personal information that I can't divulge at this time, but I'm working on some other stuff, too." I hesitated to let that sink in, then added, "I'm on the case."

Roberta stayed in the food court with the gang, while I went to the Hallmark store to get a card. I chose one with a cat face that looked exactly like Mr. Whiskers, except he was wearing a little baseball cap and sunglasses. The inside caption said, Have a purr-fect birthday! I signed my name and drew a cat's footprint on the bottom of the card, and asked Lonnie to send me pictures of the party on her phone. I left the mall and rode towards home and cut over one block to the Post Office.

After I mailed the card, I checked out the wanted posters. None of them were murderers, and that was disappointing. As part of my training, I tried to focus on a picture and remember the distinguishing characteristics of the person, like did they have scars or tattoos. I spent about fifteen minutes doing that and then rode home. Her car was still in the driveway.

When I went into the house, they were both sitting at the kitchen table drinking coffee. My dad was in his usual Saturday morning sweats. She was wearing a robe and had her hair wrapped in a towel like she had just come out of the shower. I couldn't believe it, it was 11:16 a.m. She had the robe zipped up to her neck, and I hoped she had something else on underneath it. "Sheesh!"

Dad wanted to know about my trip to the mall, and I told him about the birthday card and that I went to the P.O. to mail it. Something told me not to say anything about studying the mug shots. As a trained investigator, I was beginning to develop a suspicious sense that some things are better left unsaid.

I was upstairs when I heard Karen leave. I wanted to know if he kissed her. If he did, it was under the porch roof, and I couldn't see it. All I saw was that he carried her bag to the car and waved as she drove away. Thankfully, that was all I saw.

I was at my desk trying to make a list of cool agency names when my dad knocked on the door frame and entered. He said, "Well, ... what, do you think?"

"Um... about what, Dad?"

"Karen, what do you think of her?" Before I could answer, he added, "She thinks a lot of you."

"She's very nice. Do you like her?"

"Yes, I do. We'll be seeing a lot more of each other and give you two a chance to get to know each other."

I said, "That would be great, Dad." This time, I crossed my fingers behind my back.

"How 'bout we go out for pizza tonight?"

"That would be really great." I uncrossed my fingers before I said that.

Chapter Eight

Surveillance

I t was still warm at night, and we drove to Perry's Pizza with the top down. I wore my mother's favorite golf visor to keep my hair from blowing and played loud music on the radio. For the first time in two weeks, I felt that my dad was focused on me. It felt good. We ordered a large "Super Supreme" and a pitcher of Coke to sit there and pig out while we talked about a lot of things. I tried to understand what my dad was saying about a new relationship. I know he's lonesome, but I also know he's vulnerable right now and maybe not thinking clearly. I know my role is to protect him from himself.

I worked a few questions about Karen into the conversation, and he didn't seem suspicious about that. Now I know where she lives, where her "Manufacturer's Representative" office is, and that she was thirty-nine years old. Two years younger than my dad, the same age my mother was when she died.

After our meal, we drove down along the shore to watch the sunset, and I hadn't seen my dad look so happy in a long time. I wonder if I'm doing the right thing by investigating Karen. Part of me doesn't want to find out anything that would hurt him, but a more significant part of me feels there is something funny about this relationship. Besides, I'm sure he'd be happier with Beth.

When we got home, I went upstairs with Mr. Whiskers to research further into the new data I had just collected. I Googled her address and entered that into my Case 002 file. Then I went to Google Earth and zoomed down on her home like a hawk. It wasn't much of a house, probably two bedrooms and one bath. Not what I expected from someone who dressed as fancy as she did and drove a Cadillac. There was a single garage separate from the house, and maybe the car was in there because it wasn't showing in the driveway. A split cedar fence enclosed the backyard, but there was no dog or any kid toys. There was a similar house to the right and left of hers, and when I went to street view and panned in both directions, it looked like a development of copycat homes. The community name was Hemlock Hills. I know where that is, and I can ride there on my bike. I don't understand why it's called 'Hills,' there aren't any.

When I Googled her "business" address, I got really suspicious. There was nothing there. It was in a bad part of the city and appeared to be only a vacant lot. There was probably a building there at one time, but now only an old foundation. I went to the street view and panned around and shivered. It was scary.

I entered that information into the file, then sat there staring at the screen. My head was rapidly filling with all kinds of possibilities. But I knew one thing for sure, I needed to step up my investigation and get it done soon because I start Forensic II in two weeks, and I'm worried about my dad.

Sunday morning, I got the paper from the porch, made coffee, toasted a bagel, and spread cream cheese on that. I took this on a tray upstairs and knocked on my dad's door with my foot. He was in his bathrobe and pajamas, and his hair was still mussed, but his smile was a mile wide. "Well, thank you very much, room service, I suppose you expect a large tip for this." He sounded good.

"No, Dad, I just wanted to do this for you. I know how much you and Mom used to enjoy a lazy start on Sundays." He put a hand on my shoulder and closed his eyes. When he opened them, I saw a tear. If I didn't have the tray in front of me, I know he would have hugged me and probably cried more. I could have stayed and sat at the table to read the funnies, but I told him I needed to feed Mr. Whiskers and went back downstairs and did my own crying. I washed my eyes at the kitchen sink, got a bowl of Rice Krispies, and sat down more determined than ever that I would get to the bottom of the Karen mystery before she could do any harm.

When my dad came downstairs, he told me how great the snack was, put the plate and cup in the dishwasher, and asked me what I planned to do today. Before I could answer, He said, "I'm taking Karen for a ride in the country. Will you be alright?"

I managed to say, "Sure, Dad," before my heart dropped down into my shoes.

He asked, "What are your plans for today?"

I don't think it mattered what I said, so I answered, "Just hanging with my friends."

He reached in his pocket and, at the same time, asked, "Do you need any money?"

"I'm all set, Dad."

He took out his billfold and gave me twenty dollars saying with a chuckle, "Don't spend it all in one place."

"Thanks, Dad, what time will you be home?"

"We should be back at about four."

We, he said, we. That means Karen will be coming back with him. Will she be staying over again? Will they be in the same bedroom. These thoughts bounced around the inside of my head like a ping pong ball. Somehow, I knew when I woke up, this would be a bad day. My mood began to darken, then I remembered what Mom always said, something her mother told her, "When life gives you lemons, you can make lemonade." Or, something like that.

The balls stopped pinging and ponging, and the light bulb went on. If Dad and Karen were riding in the country, that meant no one would be home at her house. Hmmm.

I waited for a few minutes after Dad left, then packed some more snacks, my CSI kit, and the magnifying glass in my backpack. I checked the cat dishes to make sure he had water and kibble, clicked on my helmet, locked the door, and rode my bike to Karen's street. I kept a sharp eye out for my dad's car. A new red Mercedes convertible would stand out like a thumb hit with a hammer in this neighborhood.

I rode around several streets on the outskirts of the community, trying to look like I belonged there. I found Karen's house and made one more pass around the block. The house behind hers was for sale and appeared empty. I pulled into the driveway and parked my bike behind the garage. I stood there listening, and the only thing I heard was the bumping of my heart. This was my first surveillance job, and I was a little anxious. The six-foot fence top was about a foot over my head, but there was an old five-gallon plastic bucket turned upside down behind the garage, and by standing on that, I could peek over the top of the fence. Her yard was in worse shape than it appeared on Google Earth. I wish I had brought the binoculars that are in the cabinet with mom's cameras. I also wish I had brought one of those cameras. I took some pictures with my phone.

It was broad daylight, but no one seemed to be around in any direction, so I grabbed the top of the fence and pulled myself as high as I could, then on the second try, I swung a leg over the top and hooked my heel on that. Then I pulled myself up more and lay across the top. I stopped and rested a minute then tried to roll over the top, but it was harder than I thought, and I lost my grip.

I fell in a heap with the backpack under me gasping for air. I lay there for a minute, wondering if it would be fatal, or if I would survive. After a minute, I caught my breath, figured I would live, and rolled onto my hands and knees. A small bit of blood ran down my arm from a cut on my right elbow. My first investigation wound.

I looked around, and there was no one in sight. I got to my feet and leaned against the fence for a minute to get my head straight and then went quickly along the fence to the house. I stopped at the corner of the fence by the closed gate and listened for any sounds coming from the house. There were none. Curtains covered all the windows except the one on the window in the back door.

I crept to the small back porch and stopped again. Then up the three wooden stairs to the door on my hands and knees. I slowly rose up until I could see over the bottom of the window. The first thing I noticed was the yellow-painted walls that looked old and a round clock on the wall that was not showing the right time. My first thought was how Karen could live in this dump? I got a little higher and saw a kitchen table with two wooden chairs. On one of those chairs, a large sweatshirt was draped over the back, and one of the sleeves had a cuff reaching to the floor. A camo ball cap was hooked over the chair top on the other side of the table. Two beer cans were on the table.

How could Karen live here? Did I make a mistake and surveil the wrong house? I could see into part of the front room. I saw the corner of a sofa with a rip along the top and a TV set against the front wall. I tested the doorknob by gripping it with the bottom of my tee-shirt so I wouldn't leave any prints. It was locked.

I haven't learned how to pick a lock yet, and I didn't have any tools. This is something I need to get. I took out my phone to take a picture of the kitchen. Suddenly a man's tattooed arm rose above the sofa, and the TV clicked on.

I dropped down below the window, and my heart flipped into my throat. I slipped off the porch and ran to the corner of the fence to hide there behind a scraggly bush, hoping he couldn't hear my heart beats or my raspy breathing. Nothing happened

I need to get out of this enclosed yard. I crept to the gate section of the fence, quietly raised the latch and pulled. It didn't open. I tried again, harder. Was it locked? Was it stuck? I pulled back, harder, it didn't budge. I was trapped.

Chapter Nine

Discovery

I huddled back behind the bush. I needed to think. Detectives don't get scared. I asked myself what Beth would do? I began to calm down and looked around for something to climb on. On the other side of the porch, I saw the top of a metal trash can. If I could bring that over to the edge of the fence, I might be able to climb on it and then go over the fence.

I listened for any sounds coming from the house. I heard nothing, not even the TV. I crept back to the porch, grabbed the trash can handles and tried to lift it. It was heavy. I hitched up my backpack, grabbed the handles again, and managed to lift it a little and drag it back toward the fence. When I got it in position, I got one knee up on it and hoisted myself to both knees. It was wobbly. I held onto the fence and managed to stand with my hands, gripping the top of the fence. A little kid was playing with some toy trucks on the far side of the other yard

I looked back once more toward Karen's house, then hoisted myself and rolled over the top. The can tipped over with a crash, I landed on my back, and the little kid began laughing. I scrambled to my feet waved to him, and put a shush finger to my lips as I moved quickly along the fence to the row of closely planted bushes at the back of that yard. I worked my way through the bushes and ran to get my bike.

I slumped against the garage and tried to breathe. There was no sign that whoever was in Karen's house had seen or heard me. I took my helmet off the handlebar and clicked it on, mounted my bike, and rode out into the street.

No way this could this be Karen's house. I didn't like her, but she was kind of pretty and well dressed. She drove a Cadillac and worked as a Manufacturers Rep. My dad liked her. How could that be her house? Who was that man? I rode my bike back around the block to check the house number then rode home with a lot of questions swirling in my mind. Being a private investigator is hard work.

When I got home, I played with Mr. Whiskers for a few minutes, teasing him with a catnip mouse on the end of a cord, then I went to my room and opened my laptop. I checked all the information I had, everything was as I had learned it from my dad. There must be some mistake.

I was surprised but delighted when my dad came home alone. Not only happy that Karen wasn't with him but also because I could ask him some questions. I went downstairs and said, "Hi, Dad, how was your ride?"

"It was lovely, we drove up by the reservoir, and it was beautiful. How was your day?"

"It was okay, I went for a long bike ride, and then I came home and played with the cat. I've been working on my CSI stuff. Where's Karen?"

"She planned to come over, but she had an urgent call from one of her clients and had to head into her office."

"That's too bad, so you had to drive her all the way home?"

"No, I met her at the Midway Mall parking lot, that's where we always meet."

"Oh." Maybe that's the answer. "I thought you picked her up at her house."

"No, she said she was always on the go, and it was just as easy to meet halfway at the mall."

"Oh." I could see that my dad was not thinking clearly about this woman. I wondered if the "urgent call" came from a tattooed man. Tomorrow, I'll take another ride by the house, but I won't go sneaking over the back fence again. There's only so much a CSI Junior Tech can do.

***

The tattooed man sat with both arms on the table in the back booth at the Emerald Lounge, a half-empty glass of beer in front of him. The woman across from him had a glass of wine. She said, "So tell me again, you heard the trash can fall over and…"

"And I figure somebody used it to jump the fence. I heard the crash, but by the time I got out there, whoever it was had disappeared."

"Who do you think it was?"

"Karen, I have no idea. It was probably nothing. What about your ride?"

"It was okay, we went up around the reservoir, we parked at the turn-out, and I let him kiss me."

"Do you think you can get him to invest?"

"I think so, I know he's got money, and I think he's vulnerable since his wife died. What troubles me is that brat kid of his. She seems suspicious for some reason. She just went to a CSI summer camp, so maybe that's why she's acting funny. Maybe I'm making more out of it than I should, but if she gets in the way, you might have to take care of her." Karen showed her teeth when she said that.

Jerry shrugged and said, "Whatever." Then said, "Why did you give him this address?"

"My bad, Jerry, I wasn't thinking. He asked, and I told him, but he'll never come here. I'll always meet him at the mall parking lot. He seems okay with that."

Jerry twisted the corner of his mouth funnily and asked, "How much longer is this gonna take? We're running low on dough. The landlord came around again wanting another month's rent on that dump we're staying in, and the car rental outfit called again for another payment on the car. How much longer is it gonna take?"

"Soon, Jerry, soon. Gimme fifty bucks. I need to get my hair touched up, the roots are showing."

"Karen, I just told you we're getting low on money."

Karen stuck her hand out and stared at Jerry. He grumbled and took out his wallet. She said, "Thanks, now drink up. Let's get out of here, I'm tired. This scam is stressing me out, too."

***

Monday morning, I stayed in bed until I heard Dad leave, then I went downstairs with Mr. Whiskers, fed him, and got a bowl of Rice Krispies for myself. I sat there in my pajamas thinking about yesterday and shivered when I remembered the trash can tipping over and my escape. There must be a reason for this mystery. Who is Karen? I wish I could talk with Beth. When I have more evidence,

I'll go to the police station and speak with her about my suspicions. I'm not sure when I'll tell my dad.

I cleaned up the kitchen and went upstairs to get dressed. I washed off the cut on my elbow and patted on some hydrogen peroxide and replaced the band-aid I put on yesterday. The thought of my close call at Karen's house gave me a shiver. Today, I'll ride by there again and maybe go past the place where her office is supposed to be, but isn't, and take some pics. I called Roberta and asked her if she wanted to ride down there with me. I didn't tell her why.

"I can't, Ceely, my mom told me I can't go to that part of the city."

"We're not gonna stay, I just need to ride through there. It's part of an investigation."

"I still can't. You go, but be careful, call me when you get back."

"Okay." Roberta's warning should have made me think twice about doing this, but detectives can't let things like that bother them. I believe there are some important clues to be found.

I took a bottle of water to put in the holder on my bike, but I didn't take my backpack. I want to travel light in case I need to escape.

I was able to ride most of the way into the city on sidewalks and avoid the morning traffic. When I got near the location where her "office" was, there was less traffic, and I rode in the street because some of the men lounging in front of the bars looked a little creepy. I found the location and took a picture of the empty foundation, then got out of there as fast as I could.

Now, I needed to go past Karen's house and see if anything was cooking there. As I rode down her street, I saw two things that chilled me. The tattooed man was putting the trash can out at the curb for pick-up, and the Cadillac was parked in the driveway, half a block from where I was. I checked my bike mirror and swerved across the street to get as far away from the tattooed man as I could. I know he doesn't know me, but he still frightens me. I needed to get a picture, I took the phone out of my back pocket and tried to aim it as I rode by, taking a picture with my thumb. Then, I headed home as fast as I could.

I stopped my bike at the porch and ran up the stairs with my key in hand. I opened the door, stepped inside, closed and locked it, then leaned back against it breathing hard. Mr. Whiskers came softly down the hall to purr at my feet. I squatted down to stroke his silky fur and began to relax.

When I calmed down, I got a water from the fridge and a Pop-Tart. I sat at the kitchen table and opened my phone. The picture I hoped I had was worthless. It showed part of a trash can and a man's foot. I hated to think that I needed to go back and get another picture, but that's what I might have to do. This time, I'll take one of mom's cameras with a long lens and hide somewhere.

I called Roberta and told her I was home. I didn't tell her what I did, and when she said, "Wanna go to the movies with Mikey and me?" I said, "Yup."

I entered the results from my investigation today into the 002 files and made a sandwich for lunch. I wrote a note for my dad and left it on the kitchen table propped against the salt shaker, then I rode over to Roberta's house. Her mom drove us to the Cine Complex at the mall. She said she'd pick us up after the movie and I was glad of that. I'd had enough of being on my own for one day.

Chapter Ten

Suspicion

We got to the theater early. As we waited for the doors to open, I told Roberta some of what I found out. I had to tell someone. "The house was kind of dumpy. I rode around the block a couple of times and then figured out where I could hop the fence and sneak up on it. I crept up on the porch and..."

Roberta said, "Were you scared?"

"Not really, I looked in the window on the back door into the kitchen. Some guy's hat and sweatshirt were hanging from a chair, and there might have been a gun on the table, I wasn't sure."

"Wow! Was the guy there?"

"Yeah, he was in the living room, a big guy with a lot of tats on both arms, and he had a nasty scar that ran down the side of his face."

"Which side."

I rolled my eyes and said, "Does it matter?"

Roberta rolled her eyes and said, "I guess not. What else?"

"He was watching TV, and like I said, he was a big guy and had a lot of muscles, too."

"Was he smoking a cigarette?"

"I'm not sure, why, what's that got to do with anything."

Roberta made a little scrunch with the side of her mouth and said, "Nothing, I guess, I just thought all big, bad guys with a lot of tats and muscles would be smoking a cigarette." She moved out of the ticket line and started making some hip-hop moves.

"Maybe he just finished one. Sheesh!" I rolled my eyes for the second time.

"Okay, what else.?" She was trying to moonwalk.

"I took a picture with my phone."

"Let me see it." Roberta was bouncing on her toes. I dug out my phone and scrolled to the picture of the kitchen.

Roberta took the phone, looked closely, and said, "I don't see any guy."

I took it back. "He moved just before I took the picture."

"I didn't see a gun." Robbie looked like she was about to attempt a cartwheel.

I sighed and said, "I told you I wasn't sure. Anyway, now I needed to get back out of the yard, so I..."

She cut back in line and said, "Hopped the fence?"

"Not quite, the fence was much higher at the end by the house, maybe ten feet. I went back by the porch and carried the heavy metal trash can to the corner of the fence, hopped on that, and then rolled over the top landing on my feet on the other side. There was a mean-looking dog on a chain that started barking like crazy, so I got out of there as quick as I could and ran to where I hid my bike."

"Was there a fence there?"

"Oh, yeah, I forgot. It was about six feet high, so I could jump up and grab the top and pull myself over. It was easy. I didn't need a trash can."

Roberta was squinting at me. "How tall are you?"

"Five feet, one inch. Why?"

"Just figuring."

I spotted Mikey and changed the subject by calling to him. We made space in the line.

The doors opened, and we entered the theater before Roberta assaulted me with any more questions.

Roberta's mom was waiting for us when we came out and took us from there to Sammy's Ice Cream Parlor on Winthrop Street, where I had a vanilla sundae with butterscotch and marshmallow topping and whipped cream on top of that. It was a pretty good day.

***

After he set the trash can at the curb, Jerry went into the house and said, "Karen, what does that brat kid look like?"

"Which brat kid?'

"The one from the mark, Dan's kid."

"Oh, she's about this tall," Karen held a hand out at shoulder height. "Cute kid, light brown hair down to about here," the hand touched the back of her neck. "Why?"

Jerry pursed his lips and said, "Some kid just rode by here on a bike."

"So?"

"I think she tried to take a picture of me with her phone."

"What?"

"Yeah, as she rode by, she held the phone like this," Jerry put his right hand at his waist.

"Are you sure?"

"Nah, I'm making the whole thing up. Of course, I'm sure."

Karen pulled out a chair, sat down at the kitchen table, propped an elbow on the top, and rested her chin in her hand. "I told you I was suspicious about the brat. But we don't know if it's her. Let me think." Karen drummed the fingers of her left hand on the table, clicking it with her long nails. "How long was this kid's hair?"

"I don't know, she had a helmet on."

"So, it could be any kid."

"Maybe, it just seemed weird."

"Here's what I'll do, Jerry, I'll make up a story to go over to their house, and I'll get a pic of her. How's that sound."

"Good idea. When?"

Karen pointed toward the counter. "Hand me my phone."

***

Dad drove in the driveway just behind Roberta's mother and got out of his car to talk with her. Roberta and I went into the house because she hadn't seen Mr. Whiskers in a while and wanted to say hello. When she went back outside, I heard my dad come up the porch stairs, speak with Roberta a minute, then come in the house all smiles. He said, "Well, kiddo, I guess you had a good day."

I knew right away that he was having a good day because he doesn't always call me 'kiddo.'

"What's up, Dad?"

"Karen called me and suggested we have a barbeque tonight."

"Here?"

"Yup, she's coming over at six with some steaks, and I will show her why I'm called the King of the Backyard Barbecue."

I made a face and said, "Can I help?"

"Sure, kiddo, can you make a potato salad?"

"Dad, I'm thirteen and a half, almost. I was helping Mom make potato salad since I was eleven. Sheesh!"

"How 'bout a green salad?"

"Let me see what we have." I opened the fridge and took out a tomato, lettuce, celery, a cucumber, an apple, and a bottle of Ranch dressing. "We're all set."

"What about appetizers?"

I rolled my eyes and said, "I'll think of something. Calm down, King. We're all set."

My dad said, "Great! Then he bounded up the stairs like a teenager to change out of his business clothes and get his barbecue apron and tall chef's hat." I smiled and shook my head, but it was good to see my dad so happy. I just wish he was happy with Beth instead of Karen.

She arrived at 6:30. Dad met her at her car. She gave him a kiss on the cheek then handed him a bag with the steaks and a big bag of cheese curls. "Yuck!"

She said to me, "How nice to see you again, Celia. Won't this be fun?" She was showing a lot of teeth when she smiled.

"Yes, Karen, it will be great." Then I added, "I made potato salad, just like my mom did." But she was walking away, and I don't think she heard me.

I took a basket with the outdoor plates and cutlery to the patio table in the backyard and laid out three place settings. Karen came out with glasses and a bottle of wine for her and Dad, then said, "This is so lovely, let me get a picture of this. Stand by the table, Celia."

I did, and she snapped a picture with her phone. "That is so cute, Celia. Now stand over there by the tree."

I did, only this time, instead of smiling, I made a face. Karen said, "Oh, what a lovely picture. Now why don't you put your bike helmet on, and we'll take one more. That will be adorable."

What? Why does she want a bike helmet picture? I was starting to not like this, but my dad heard her say it and said, "That will be adorable, Ceely."

My bike was parked by the porch. I sulked my way over there, took the helmet off the handlebars, and clicked it on my head. I stood there with my arms folded across my chest and a sour look on my face. Karen took the picture gushing over how adorable it was, and my dad agreed. Sheesh!

Karen put her phone away after showing the pictures to my dad. I said, "I don't need to see them, Karen, I know what I look like." Then I went into the house to get a Coke and think about what just happened.

Chapter Eleven
Jerry the Moke

P rivate investigators have a sixth sense that tells them something is not right. We rely on that faculty to solve crimes and stay out of danger. I felt uneasy with the picture taking. Karen seemed to have a particular reason to record me. Something was bothering me, but I couldn't bring it into focus. When I go to bed tonight, I'll lay there with Mr. Whiskers beside me and think about this. I know there's more to it, I just don't know what right now. Maybe later.

My dad did a great job cooking the steaks wearing his silly apron and tall chef's hat. Karen praised my potato salad, and I really think she meant it. One small checkmark in the good column for her. But the bad column was filling up rapidly. I told Dad I would clean up, while he and Karen sat on the chaise lounges and reached across to hold hands as the sun was dropping below the maple trees. Yuck!

I put on my pajamas, brushed my teeth, and went to bed early to lay there with Mr. Whiskers at my side and my earbuds softly playing Taylor Swift songs.

I replayed the afternoon picture taking. Karen there with her thin smile saying how cute and adorable it was, my dad agreeing with her, and my feeling that something was not right.

Boing! Suddenly, I had a scary thought. Had the tattooed man seen me take a picture of him? I replayed that scene in my head. How I rode by, how I held the phone. Did I look at him? Did he look at me? This is getting serious. I need a plan. I finally fell asleep, knowing precisely what I would do.

I had a dream. I was riding my bike. When I looked in the handlebar mirror, I saw the tattooed man coming after me. I pedaled as fast as I could, but I went slower and slower. Then I started going backward. He ran up beside me. Now, I knew where I'd seen him before. He grabbed my hair…

I woke up in a fright with Mr. Whiskers pawing at my hair. Phew! That was scary. I got up and went downstairs with the cat trailing at my heels. Dad was already at the breakfast table, eating a bagel and drinking his coffee. "Morning, Dad."

"Good morning, Ceely. Sleep well?"

"Sure, until Whiskers started pulling at my hair. He wants his breakfast."

Dad laughed, then asked, "What are your plans for today?"

"Nothing much, call Robbie, maybe ride bikes, go to the mall, I don't know." I reached in the cupboard for the cat food. "What about you, Dad?"

"I'm meeting Karen at Starbucks for an early coffee. She has an interesting proposal for an investment she wants to show me. Something about a new product she's going to be representing. She said I might want to get in on the 'ground floor' with this thing."

I hate it when my dad makes air quotes, he looks silly. "Gee, that sounds great." I put the cat dish on the floor and reached for my Rice Krispies.

Dad got up and put his dishes in the dishwasher, kissed the top of my head, said, "Stay out of trouble." And left.

I sat there wondering if he had his "head on straight," as Mom used to say.

Robbie called me before I called her. "What are you doing today, wanna go to the mall?"

"Maybe later, I'm working on a case this morning, wanna come?"

"Wow! Where are you going?"

"First, I'm going to the Post Office…"

Robbie made a smirky noise and said, "That's no big deal."

"…then I'm going to the Police Station."

"Wow!" That got her attention. "Yeah, I'll come over. Ta."

"Ta?"

"I'm reading this British book, and that's what one of the characters says. I'm not sure what it means, but it sounds cool."

"Okay, I'll see you. Get here as soon as you can. I have a busy schedule. Ta." I picked up Whiskers and began petting him on my lap.

***

Karen closed the prospectus and said, "What about it, Dan, I'm trying to get you in on the ground floor."

Dan nodded and tilted his head a little. "Yes, Karen, it all sounds good; believe me, I'm interested. But, a hundred thousand dollars is a lot of money." He steepled his hands with his elbows on the table.

Karen took another drink from her Mocha Cappuccino, pursed her lips, tilted her head, and said, "It is, Dan, but the rewards are huge. You can see that, can't you?"

"Absolutely, let me think about it, and we'll talk about it again, Thursday. I may be bringing you a big check." Dan reached across the small round table and put a hand on top of hers. He looked into her eyes and smiled.

Karen smiled back, put her other hand on top of his, and said, "Please do, you won't regret it."

***

Robbie and I took the back road to the Post Office so we could ride in the street. Inside, I went directly to the bulletin board and stared at the pictures. I pointed to the one at the top left and said, "That might be the guy."

"Robbie said, "Wow!"

In the picture, he had a beard, when I saw him on the street, he didn't. But I'm sure it was him, he had mean eyes. I read the description, WANTED for Bank Fraud, Embezzlement, Robbery: Gerald Marven, alias Jerry Maxwell, Jerry Morgan, Jerry the Moke.

Robbie said, Wow! What's a moke?"

"I don't know, I think it means he's very dangerous."

"Wow!"

I read the description giving his height, weight, hair color, eye color, and it said both arms were heavily tattooed. "That's the guy."

I took a picture of the poster as a clerk came out of the side office door and said, "What are you kids doing?"

"I'm working on a school project. Sir."

"Okay, don't mess with anything."

"No, Sir."

He went back into the office, and Robbie said, "What a jerk."

We carefully rode to the downtown Police Station on the sidewalks. The traffic this time of day was heavy. We stacked our bikes in the rack at the right side of the steps. Robbie said, "Do you think we should lock them?"

I gave her a look and said, "Have you ever heard of a bike being stolen from the Police Station?"

"I guess not."

We climbed the three wide granite steps into the lobby. On the right side of the small room was a wooden bench. Robbie sat there, bouncing her feet on the floor. On the left side was a thick glass window with a speaker below it. A police officer sat behind the glass closely watching us. He said, "Good morning, Ladies, how may I help you?"

I stepped to the window and read the small sign to the right of the speaker. To talk, press and hold the red button. To listen, release.

I pressed and said, "Sir, I'd like to speak with Beth... er, Detective Lieutenant Frankel, please."

He looked down at something and then, "Lieutenant Frankel is on vacation, she won't be back until Thursday." Then he looked over his shoulder and back at me. "Sergeant Bertrando is here, can she help you?"

"I pressed the button again, "No, thank you, Sir. I'll come back Thursday."

He smiled and said, "Would you care to leave a message?"

Button again. "Please tell Beth that Celia was here."

He asked me how to spell that, and I answered C-E-L-I-A. I'm a CSI Junior Tech, Sir."

He smiled again and said," I'm pleased to meet you, Junior Tech Celia, I'll be sure she gets the message. Take care, Ladies."

Robbie and I waved to him and left.

When we got outside, I said, "What did you think of that, pretty impressive, huh?"

She made a little scrunch with her mouth and said, "Not really." And then we rode to the mall.

Chapter Twelve
Bug in a Rug

Jerry rotated the phone into landscape view as if that would make a difference. Karen said, Well?"

"Yeah, that could be her."

Karen glared at him, "Could be? Is it or isn't it? We need to move fast."

"Yeah, that's her." He handed back the phone. "What now?"

"You need to snatch her?"

Jerry sat up straighter, shook his head sharply, and said, "What?"

"You heard me. We need to kidnap her and hold the brat somewhere until I can close this deal. I think she's on to us. The little brat."

"I'm glad you said, we, Karen, but it's still kidnapping, that's serious."

"Jerry, we'll take her phone, lock her in the basement, or something, give her some video games and a bunch of snacks, and she'll be alright. I'm meeting with Dan again, Thursday, and that should do the trick. We'll do it Thursday morning and bring her here. I'm meeting Dan for lunch; once I get that check, we're out of here."

Jerry rubbed his chin and said, "What's the plan?"

Karen pursed her lips and said, "Here's what I'm thinking. Hire a panel van with a sliding side door, no windows in the back. We'll wait for her to leave her house and pull up beside her. I'll be disguised and ask her something, like have you seen my lost dog or something. You'll sneak around the van, throw a blanket over her head, throw her in the side door, and duct tape her. Easy peasy."

"What? That's a stupid idea." Jerry sat there, shaking his head. "You think she'll just stand there and let me put a blanket over her head?"

"Stupid yourself, Jerry, look at you, you've got muscles on your muscles. You can't handle an eighty-pound kid? I'm ashamed of you, Jerry, I thought you were a big, strong guy. That's what I liked about you, Jerry" Karen reached across the table and put a hand on his arm while she looked directly in his eyes and smiled. "Am I wrong, Jerry," she asked in a low sexy voice.

"Okay, but we don't have any duct tape." When Jerry said that, Karen removed her hand and rolled her eyes.

***

We finally got some rain. It poured all day Wednesday and flooded some of the streets, an excellent day to stay inside and read. I was reading another book by Alan Bradley about Flavia De Luce, the eleven-year-old English girl solving crimes and getting kidnapped and stuff like that. I was propped up in my bed on a bunch of pillows with Mr. Whiskers snuggled against my bare feet. My earbuds were playing Ariana Grande, and I had a bag of dried apple slices at my side. It doesn't get any better than this. Then the phone vibrated in my lap — ROBERTA.

"Hey."

"Hey, back at you."

"What are you doing?"

"Calling you."

I scratched the top of my head. "I know that. I mean, why?"

"Do you want to go to the mall? "

"It's raining."

"I know that. I mean later."

I don't know, maybe."

"Okay."

"Okay." We ended that conversation, and I went back to reading about this brilliant young girl with her adventures and crime-solving and harrowing escapes. Sheesh!

When my dad came home later in the afternoon, he was all excited and said we should go out for some pizza again. I was all into that. He told me he had been talking with Karen about some business thing where he would invest a lot of money, but that it could be a good thing because his "return on equity would be very favorable." I assume that meant he would make a lot more than he put into it. I said, "That's nice, can we get a double cheese and pepperoni with lots of onions?"

When we got home, Dad went right into his study and began reading the prospectus that Karen gave him. He said that it contained all the information about the new company, and he wanted to understand it so he could make up his mind. He was meeting her for lunch tomorrow, Thursday. The day Beth returned from vacation.

I called Robbie and asked her if she wanted to ride to the Police Station with me tomorrow, and she was all in for that. "I'll meet you in front of my house, nine o'clock, don't be late."

She said, "Ciao."

"What?"

"I'm reading a book about Italy, they say that all the time. See ya tomorrow. Ciao"

I said, "Ta," and hung up.

***

When I came downstairs Thursday morning, my dad was at the kitchen table with his coffee and an empty plate that had a few toast crumbs on it. He had a yellow pad and pen to the side, and the prospectus open in front of him.

"Hey, Dad, what's up?"

"'Morning, kiddo, just going over this deal one more time. I'm gonna do it. It's a lot of money, but it looks good to me and, of course, it will be good for you. You'll be going to college in a few years and probably graduate school after that, and we're looking at a lot of expense. It would be nice to have that covered."

"But, Dad, how do you know it's a good thing? I mean, how well do you know Karen? I mean, maybe she's not telling you the truth about all this. I've been doing some investigating, and I think…"

My dad looked at his watch and said, "I've gotta run, kiddo, hold that thought, I need to get to the office early." He kissed the top of my head and left in a rush before I could tell him what I know. I'm glad Beth will be back today, and I can tell her. She'll know what to do.

I cleaned up the kitchen, made my bed, got dressed, put on my new pink Nike hi-tops, pinned my CSI Junior Tech badge to my shirt, played with Whiskers, and went out front with my bike to wait for Roberta. We live on a short side street with very little traffic, especially in the morning. The sky had cleared, and the rain had left everything bright and shining. It all smelled clean and fresh. A gray panel van turned down our street and went by me.

"That's her, Jerry, turn around." Karen reached into the bag at her feet and took out a large red wig and an oversized pair of dark sunglasses. Jerry made a U-turn at the end of the block and drove up to the curb beside Celia. "Miss, excuse me miss. Ah, 'm looking for my lost dog. Have y'all seen him?" Karen held a picture out the window she had cut out of a magazine so Celia could see it and spoke with an exaggerated southern accent.

I put the kickstand down and went to the van. Maybe I can use my detecting skills and get another client. I'll call it The Lost Dog Case, number 003. I looked at the picture of a beagle that seemed like it had been cut out of a magazine dog food ad.

Suddenly, I saw in the side mirror part of a tattooed arm, something gray and then nothing, as a blanket was thrown over my head. Oh crap! I'm being kidnapped!

***

Joe Ritacco, the accountant, was drumming a ballpoint pen on the edge of his desk as he flipped the pages of a prospectus with his other hand. Dan was standing in front of the desk, shifting his weight from one foot to the other, anxious for Joe's response. "Well, Joe, what do you think?"

Joe closed the folder, leaned back in his swivel chair, and said, "It's a lot of money, Dan."

"I know, I suppose there is some risk, but that's true with everything. Karen assures me this is a good thing."

Joe began swiveling his chair left and right. "How well do you know this Karen, Dan."

"Actually, Joe, we're getting pretty tight with each other. She stayed over the other night, and I like her a lot. I think she likes Celia, too. We're talking about getting engaged."

Joe started rubbing his chin. He made a funny little tightness with the corner of his mouth whenever he was thinking about difficult things. Finally, he said, "Well, Dan, it's your money. If that's what you want, I'll tell Norma to call the bank, and we'll get you a cashier's check."

"Thanks, Joe, this will work out just fine. I can feel it."

***

I was lifted off the ground with my arms pinned to my side. I was screaming inside a woolen blanket and kicking with my hi-tops against his legs. I heard the side van door open, and I was thrown inside. Then I heard a ripping sound, like duct tape being peeled from a roll. It was duct tape, and they were wrapping it around the blanket, pinning my arms to my sides. Then they taped my ankles, and I felt like I'd been rolled inside a rug.

The southern voice said, "Hold still kid. I'm gonna cut an air hole in the blanket so you can breathe." It sounded like Karen's voice. I suddenly realized I was having trouble breathing and began to panic.

Her hand searched the blanket for my nose, and she said again, "Hold still." I felt the cold scissors against the side of my nose, then a rush of fresh air, and I had a hole that freed up my nose and mouth. Now I could breathe. Now I needed to think. Screaming wouldn't do any good. The van turned a sharp corner, and I rolled and crashed into the side of the van. This is not good. I squirmed my body, so I was lying across the van. Then it came to a sudden stop, and I crashed into the back of the front seats. It started abruptly again, and I rolled to the back and crashed into the rear doors. This is definitely not good.

By the time the van came to its final stop, I felt like I was a tennis ball that had been volleyed back and forth over a net.

Chapter Thirteen
HELP!

T he van bumped over the curb and drove up a driveway and stopped quickly. I hit my head on the seats again. The sliding door opened, and somebody grabbed me and dragged me outside then threw me over a shoulder. I assume it was Tattoo Man. I heard an outside bulkhead open, and the doors slap against the house, then we went downstairs into a musty, smelly basement. He flipped me off his shoulder with a grunt then laid me on the floor. I heard someone else, probably the woman come down the stairs.

When she spoke in her phony southern accent and said, "We're gonna keep you here for a few hours y' all, then we're gonna let you loose like a muskrat from a box of rotten apples. Got it y'all?"

I spat some lint out of my mouth and said, "Yup."

"Alright, y'all just lay here quiet like a bug in a rug, and we'll be back to let you go in a few hours."

I heard her walk away, and I said, "Is that you, Karen?"

She stopped and said, "No, y'all." Then she went back up the stairs.

I heard her heels clicking on the floor and the man's heavy steps as they went out the back kitchen door. Then I listened to the metal bulkhead doors close, and the van drove away. Behind that, another car drove away. I assumed that was Karen's Cadillac. I was in a tight spot, but I was feeling good about my deductive skills. Now all I needed was to get out of here. I screamed as loud as I could, "HELP!"

I did that for a few minutes, and then my throat was dry, so I decided to use common sense detective methods to escape. Before they duct-taped me, I remembered something Flavia de Luce did when her sisters tied her up and left her in a closet.

She steepled her fingers, so when they bound her wrists, and she relaxed, there was a slight space in the bindings. I had angled my elbows out a little, so when they were relaxed, the blanket was not so tight. I braced my feet against a wall and tried to squirm my way out of the blanket. That didn't work. I squiggled my body around and searched along the wall with my bound feet. I felt a pipe that came up out of the floor and ran up the wall.

There was an object on the pipe with a lever that felt like maybe a valve or something. I hooked my ankles over that and tried pulling the duct tape off. The handle moved, and I heard water running onto the floor. It began to wet the blanket. I tried to lift my feet off the valve, but they were caught on something. My legs were suspended off the floor, and the water had reached the bottom of my head. If this kept up, the small basement would flood, and I would drown. I began screaming for help again.

***

As usual, Roberta was late, when she rounded the corner on her bike and saw Celia's bike there on the sidewalk, she wiped a hand across her sweaty face and figured Celia had gone back into the house for a minute. She went up on the porch and rang the doorbell. No answer. She walked around the back of the house, and no one was there. She sat on the front step to think about her next move.

***

Detectives don't cry. Detectives don't panic. They think. They act. They get out of tight jams. I spread my arms as wide as I could and raised them as far as my face. I tried to rip the breathing hole open and managed a small tear in the old blanket. The water was touching the back edge of my ears. I lifted my head up and could see my legs suspended in the air.

I brought my hands up to the hole to try again and felt my metal CSI Junior Tech badge. I unpinned it, brought it to the edge of the tear, and began sawing at the fabric. The rip got longer.

I sawed faster and soon could reach one hand outside the hole. I had to let my head fall back into the water to give me more space to work for my hand. I got one arm out of the hole and began sawing at the duct tape. The water was running in my ears. I need to move faster.

***

Roberta called Celia and got her voicemail. What else to do. She thought about calling Dan, but she didn't have his number or know the name of his company. She knew where it was and decided to ride over there. Maybe that's where Celia was.

***

I got through several wraps of the tape and began yanking at one end, the tape peeled away, but there was still one more layer, and I sawed frantically. The water was getting near my cheekbones. The blanket was getting heavy. I was shivering from the cold water. I sawed more and felt the last layer of the tape part, and the blanket loosened. Now I had to work the rolls of the blanket off me and get to my feet. I rolled back and forth on the floor, splashing in the water, and the blanket kept loosening. I was able to sit up and see the valve. My shoelace had caught in the handle and pulled it down, letting the water rush out of the opened outlet. I moved my butt closer to the wall and pushed my feet back up, and the water stopped. I was exhausted, my head fell back into the water, and it rose to just below my nose.

I rested a minute, then carefully lifted my ankles to get the shoelace loop off the valve handle. I sat up in the water, unwound the tape wrapped around my ankles, and stood up. My legs were shaking. I got as far as the basement stairs and had to sit down and rest. Suddenly, the thought of my near-drowning hit me, and I cried into my hands. Sometimes, detectives get emotional, and there's nothing wrong with that. After a minute, I dried my eyes with the back of my hand and walked up the stairs with my wet sneakers squishing on the wooden steps.

I found a glass, filled it with water, and sat at the kitchen table to get my thoughts straight. I had no phone. They must have grabbed that out of my back pocket when they rolled me in the blanket. My grandparents have a thing called a landline that has a dial on it with finger holes to make phone calls. I searched for one in the house, and there was none.

I thought about going to a neighbor's house and ask to call 911, but this was a bad neighborhood. I didn't know who was friendly with Karen, or the Tattooed Man. I decided to walk.

***

Karen put the check in her bag next to Celia's phone, and said, "You won't regret this, Dan. I'm sorry I've got to run, I have two other appointments today. Can we get together tomorrow night? It's Friday, Dan, no work on Saturday. We can sleep in." She got up, kissed his cheek, and left the restaurant with a big smile on her face.

***

I squished down the sidewalk, walking as fast as I could in the wet clothes, heading toward the Police Station. A car pulled up at the curb, and I jumped a mile. Some guy yelled, "Hey, kid, wanna ride?" I started running. He drove past me and blew the horn. Creep!

When I got out of the bad neighborhood, I began to relax as I got closer to the station, closer to Beth.

***

Roberta parked her bike outside Eastern Metals Machining, Inc. and pulled open the all-glass door. A woman behind a desk across the lobby smiled and said, "How can I help you, Miss. The nameplate on her desk said, Norma Taylor.

"My name is Roberta, I need to speak with Celia's father, please, it's kind of important." Roberta was shifting her weight from foot to foot.

Norma said, "He's not back from lunch yet. You can sit over there and wait if you like." She pointed to some chairs behind a low table covered with magazines. "Would you like a Coke or maybe a juice if we have it?"

"No, thank you. I'll just wait." Roberta sat with her hands in her lap, bouncing her heels on the floor.

A few minutes later, the desk phone beeped. Norma answered. "Hi, Dan, there's a young lady out here that would like to speak with you. Her name is Roberta." She hung up the phone and said, "He'll be right out, Roberta."

The door behind her opened, and Dan entered the lobby. "Hi, Roberta, what can I do for you? Where's Celia?"

Roberta got to her feet and said, "I don't know, and I'm worried."

"What? Why are you worried, has she been hurt?' Dan crossed the lobby with a worried face.

"I don't know, but yesterday we went to the Post Office, and she showed me the tattooed man, and then we went to the Police Station, and she wanted to talk to Beth and tell her something, but Beth wasn't there, so we went home."

Dan motioned to Roberta to sit in a chair and sat beside her, leaning forward. "Wait a minute, Roberta, what's this about a tattooed man?"

"He's the man in the house with the gun, where Celia hopped over the fence."

"What house? What gun?" What more can you tell me, Roberta?" Dan put a comforting hand on Roberta's arm.

"I don't know where the house is, but Celia said she was investigating it and she took some pictures, they're on her phone."

"What did the pictures show?"

"She took one through the back window into the kitchen. There was a table and a chair with a man's sweatshirt hanging off it. Celia said she thought there was a gun on the table, but I didn't see it. And she took one picture looking into the living room, and you could see a guy's arm, and it had all tattoos on it. That's how she knew the guy at the post office was the same guy."

Dan's eyes got wide, and he said, "Someone working at the Post Office?"

"No, the picture on the bulletin board, Jerry the Moke."

Dan almost laughed, but he now knew what Roberta was saying. Celia was investigating a wanted criminal.

Dan stood up, "Come on, Roberta, let's go to the Police Station. Norma, have Billy take Roberta's bike to my house, she can pick it up there. Let's go."

Chapter Fourteen
Case Closed

"Wow!" Roberta said as they climbed into the leather seats of the red Mercedes. The top was down, and she took off her bike helmet and let the wind blow through her hair. Ten minutes later, they were at the station and ran up the stairs.

The same officer was behind the glass as was there the last time. He recognized Roberta, but the man rushed to the speaker and pushed the button. "I'm Celia's father, I think there's a problem, I need to speak to a detective named Beth. My daughter knows her. It's urgent."

"One moment, Sir." The officer picked up a phone and spoke into it, but Dan couldn't hear the message. When he put the phone down, he spoke through the speaker and said, "Please, have a seat, Sir, Detective Lieutenant Frankel will be right out."

Roberta was seated on the bench, heels pumping off the floor. Dan began pacing the small room.

***

I was gasping for breath, so tired, I thought I would fall on my face. I stopped running and bent over with my hands on my knees. Only a little farther. I started walking again, my hi-tops not squishing as much as before, and my wet clothes were drying and sticking to my body. Three more blocks. Two more blocks. One more... I saw a little red convertible parked in front of the Police Station and began running, with tears streaming down my face.

***

The door at the back of the lobby opened, and Beth stepped into the room. She was wearing her tailored blue business suit, tall, smiling, and her hair was done in a French Twist. She extended her hand and said, "I'm Beth Frankel, I'm delighted to meet you." She looked at Roberta on the bench and then said, "Where's Celia," as a concerned look came over her face.

Dan shook her hand while he said, "We think she's been kidnapped."

Beth lost her smile and put on her business face. "Let's go back to my office." She held open the door, and Dan and Roberta passed through.

In the detective's bullpen, they sat in Beth's glass-enclosed office near the windows. Dan began telling Beth what he and Roberta feared. About Celia's investigation and the house. When he spoke about the wanted poster,

Beth turned to her computer and made a few keystrokes. She turned the monitor so Dan and Roberta could see it. Roberta pointed at the screen and shouted, "That's him, that's the guy, Jerry the Moke."

"Oh yes, Gerald Marven, we got a tip he was in the area, and that means trouble. Do you know where that house is, Roberta?"

"No, only that Ceely said it was in a bad neighborhood. She took some pictures through the back window and one of the tattooed man in front of the house while he was putting the trash out at the curb."

Beth said, "Hmm. What day was this, Roberta?"

Roberta thought for a minute and said, Tuesday, I guess."

Beth turned to her computer, tapped on the keyboard and said, "Trash collection the next day on Wednesday would be in the Hemlock Hills section of the city. Well, that helps narrow it down a little."

Then she turned to Dan and said, "I know this will be hard for you, but go home and wait. We assume there will be a call for a ransom. Listen to their demands and tell them you'll comply, but you need to get to a bank. Stall them as much as possible without being obvious. Take notes, what did they say, how did they sound, were there any other sounds in the background you could identify.

Then call me immediately." She handed Dan a card. "This has my cell phone number on it, call me anytime day or night."

Beth stood up and extended her hand again, "I wish I could tell you more, Dan, but we're on this. I'll issue an APB with her description. I know your daughter very well." Their hands lingered as she gazed into Dan's eyes.

Beth escorted them back to the lobby, and as they entered that room, the outside door burst open.

***

With the one-hundred-thousand-dollar check in her bag, Karen left the restaurant and called Jerry, "I've got it. I'll drive directly to the airport, you take a cab. I'll get tickets for the first flight leaving for Mexico. If you get there before me, wait in the main terminal. We did it, Baby, we did it." After saying that, Karen drove to the Greyhound bus terminal, leaving the rented Caddy at the back of the lot with the key in the ignition switch. She purchased a one-way ticket to Boston, Massachusetts, where she would enter a small office on Commonwealth Avenue and have the check deposited to her personal offshore account in the Cayman Islands. Then take another bus to Portland, Maine, buy a car, and drive to the safety of Canada using a passport in her real name, Lynette Duhamel.

***

"Daddy!"

"Ceely!"

I ran across the lobby and jumped into my dad's open arms. He hugged and twirled me around in circles, too happy to say anything but, "Ceely, Ceely, Ceely."

Beth looked on with a mile-wide smile, so happy that I was safe.

Roberta was looking for space to do a cartwheel.

When Dad stopped twirling, I ran to Beth and hugged her with all my might. I'm safe now with her and Dad, and I can tell her about my investigation.

When everything calmed down, Beth said, "Well, now that you're safe, we have some work to do. Come on back into my office. Beth held the door while Dan walked through with his arm around my shoulder. Roberta followed moon-walking backward. Beth closed the door then said to a uniformed officer, "Denise, please get some Cokes for the girls and a police jacket for Celia, she's shivering."

We went into her glass-enclosed office at the back of the detective's bullpen where four other people were working in their cubicles. Beth pulled another chair over by her desk and said, How 'bout a coffee, Dan?"

"I'd love one."

Beth went to a table at the back of the bullpen and made two coffees with the Keurig machine.

Denise returned with the Cokes and a blue nylon windbreaker that had POLICE written on the back in large yellow letters.

Beth spoke over the top of her cup, "Okay, folks, let's get into this. Celia, tell me what you know, what happened?"

I told her everything from the time I started investigating Karen. I told about the surveillance I did on the house and about the wanted poster in the Post Office and that I was sure that the man who grabbed me was Jerry the Moke. I told about being wound up in the duct-taped blanket and how I thought I was gonna drown. Beth was listening intently, while her fingers were typing on a keypad. I told her how I used my CSI Junior Tech badge to cut through the tape and escape.

I stopped to take a drink of Coke, and Beth turned her Monitor to face me and said, "Is this the man who kidnapped you?"

I looked at the picture for a minute, then said, "I think so, but he didn't have a beard."

She made a few more keystrokes, and the beard disappeared. "That's him!" I shouted, pointing at the screen. She called someone and told them to put out an APB on Jerry the Moke.

She turned to me and said, "Good. Now how 'bout this picture?" She tapped the keyboard a few more times, and a woman's picture came on the screen."

"That's her! Except she's got blonde hair now, with brown roots." I was beginning to feel that I was directly involved in the investigation. I sat up straighter and hugged the police jacket around me.

My dad looked anxious to say something, but he waited for Beth to continue as he sat on the edge of the chair.

"Excellent," Beth said. "Lynette Duhamel. She has a lengthy record of crimes in Washington State. I guess she thought she could do the same out here. She didn't know we had a CSI Junior Tech on the case." Beth extended her hand and smiled. We shook hands, and I felt the warmth and strength in her grip as she smiled at me and then at my dad.

Dad pointed to the screen and said, "She took a one-hundred-thousand-dollar check from me an hour ago. I guess I was stupid and bought into her phony investment scheme. We had lunch at Maxwell's, and she drove away in a light blue Cadillac. It may have been a rental. Does that help?"

Beth picked up the phone again and talked to someone saying, "This is Lieutenant Frankel, I want an immediate APB on Lynette Duhamel, her stats are in the fugitive file. This is urgent, check all travel venues: airport, trains, and bus terminal. I repeat this is urgent. Get back to me with anything you find. She's driving a light blue Cadillac, possible rental. Have the nearest cruiser stop at Maxwell's and check the CCTV to see if we can get a plate number. Get back to me ASAP. Thanks." Then she turned to my dad and said, "We'll set a net over the entire city, she won't get far. Your information is beneficial."

When I told them about my walk from the house to the Police Station, Dad said, "Why didn't you call me, or 911?"

"They took my phone."

Beth surprised me when she said, "Excellent!" Then she asked for my number, wrote it on a pad, and picked up her phone again to call someone. "This is Lieutenant Frankel. I want a location on this phone. It may take us to Jerry the Moke or Lynette Duhamel" She gave the number, then added, "This is urgent."

When it was time to leave, Robbie and I headed for the door. Beth told me to keep the jacket, I had earned it. My dad stayed behind for a few minutes to talk with Beth and thank her.

Robbie and I waited in the lobby. I was so tired, I sat on the bench. The officer behind the glass saluted me. Robbie was moonwalking around the small room.

When we drove home, Dad dropped Robbie at her house and said he'd put her bike in our garage for the night. At home, I ran up the porch stairs, opened the door, and picked up Mr. Whiskers to hold him close against my chest. I was home, I was safe, I helped solve a crime.

When Dad came into the house, I put the cat down and hugged him again. "I said, "Isn't Beth wonderful?"

He hesitated a minute and said, "Yes, she is."

"Isn't she beautiful?"

"Yes, she is."

"She looks a lot like Mom. Doesn't she?"

"She does."

"Will you see her again?"

Dad didn't hesitate, "Whoa, Ceely. After my experience with Karen, I don't think I'm gonna be rushing into any relationships quite so soon. Remember what Mom always said, 'Once burned, shame on you…'"

"I know, Dad, I was just wondering." I put the cat down and went upstairs to get a hot shower and some clean clothes, wishing he had a better answer.

When I came downstairs, Dad was talking on the phone. I only heard his side of the conversation.

"That's wonderful, so she got as far as Boston, uh-huh, and you got the check... fantastic!" Dad smiled at me and punched the air. "What about the guy, Jerry, something...?"

"Great, and you got Ceely's phone?" He made a thumbs-up sign to me. "Wonderful, she'll be happy to get it back. You will? That's great, we'll look forward to seeing you again. How 'bout at five o'clock? But I must warn you, bring a big appetite because I am the King of the Backyard Barbecue."

Dad turned to me and said with a big smile, "Beth is bringing your phone and my check tomorrow night and staying for dinner. I'll wear my apron and the tall chef's hat."

I've never been so happy in my entire life.

I remember what my mother always said, "I see great things." Thank you, Mom.

END